THE DARKEST FLAME

ROADMAP TO YOUR HEART SERIES, BOOK #1

BY CHRISTINA LEE

This is for all the lovely folks who messaged me after reading THERE YOU STAND and insisted Vaughn and Smoke get their own story.

Cory and Jude approve.

OTHER TITLES BY CHRISTINA LEE

CHAPTER ONE
VAUGHN

"Bottoms up." I poured tequila in the three shot glasses in front of me. "Extra limes if you need 'em."

The president of the Disciples of the Road, his second in command, Jonas, and Fish, from the Scorpions Motorcycle Club, were toasting to whatever the hell they'd agreed upon in that back room.

I might've only been an honorary Disciples member because I managed their bar, the Hog's Den, but I was party to more insider information than most. We had mutual trust, and I'd put my life on the line for them if it ever came to that.

Malachi, otherwise known as Mal or Prez, had been trying to clean up the club for years while still having his hand in the most lucrative trade—auto parts. A difficult feat for sure. If he screwed the wrong people, they'd want payback. That was the way things worked in their world.

"Vaughn," Mal said after he slung back the bitter liquid and winced at the burn. "One more hit."

"Better watch your liquor, old man," I said, and Mal laughed at my ribbing. He looked lighter tonight than he had in weeks. He was always stressed about club business and protecting his men.

I grabbed the bottle on the lower shelf again. "Coming right up."

One late night a couple years back, Mal had confessed his history over a beer. How his former old lady had been strung out on meth and how he needed to do something about it or he'd lose more of the people he loved.

Mal had never seen eye to eye with his father, who had gotten the club involved in the arms and drug trade two decades ago. His father had been not only a ruthless president but also an addict, and in the end he'd paid with his own life. Since then, Mal had strategically pulled out of all illegal drug activity and was now attempting to tidy up some other things as well.

"Jude, order's up," I called across the bar. A brown takeout bag sat on the counter, and the familiar scent of Hog's Den wings wafted up my nose.

Warmth reflected in Mal's eyes before he looked back and smirked. Jude was racking up the balls for another game of pool with his boyfriend, Cory. Those two had definitely softened the prez this past year. He still felt responsible for them, as did the other guys, even though they were no longer under his charge.

When Jude waved and whispered close to Cory's ear, something burned hot in my chest. Their quiet affection seeped inside my bones as I imagined being as out as they were.

Screw that. I'd lose the respect of the club if I confessed how much I enjoyed the company of both men and women.

As a general rule, MCs were old school—barely allowing women into their fold, let alone queers. Though if there were any hope, this club would be the one to break ranks. Mal was a decent man with a good heart beneath the tough exterior. But he had enough on his plate as it was. So I'd keep my preferences discreet.

As if to muddy my illusions further, Smoke swung through the door, the guy of my goddamn fantasies. Fuck, he was a sight to behold with those hard guns, tight jeans, and his leather cut with the word *recruit* stitched above his heart.

I'd wanted to bang him the minute he stepped foot in my bar with his messy blond hair that curled over his ears, his beautiful pout, and strong fingers that I figured would feel amazing wrapped around my cock.

Add in the incident at the compound a few months back and I was a goner.

I'd attended a party and stayed overnight, too tired and drunk to drive home. In the morning, I'd jumped in the shower for a quick pick-me-up before hitting the road, and walked out to a stunned Smoke, who had stepped inside the bathroom to take a piss.

His gaze had deliberately scanned the front of me, and fuck if my cock didn't fill instantly, slapping against my abdomen. "Sorry," he mumbled, backing out of the room. I'd never spent the night out there again.

Smoke high-fived Cory and Jude at the pool table. He'd grown close to the couple after he became Jude's watchdog for months on end due to a situation involving some Latino gunrunners. Then he headed over to his leaders sitting at the corner of the bar.

I raised the bottle of tequila in a silent question. Smoke lifted his hand to swear me off, so I replaced the bottle on the shelf. He didn't drink much, actually not at all that I noticed, which made him more of a mystery.

I was curious about his story. It might've helped lessen the intrigue surrounding him. But I was too much of a chicken-shit to get that close, especially after he'd seen how my cock had responded to him while his club brothers were awake in the next room.

He'd been through some fucked up shit, I'd heard. I still didn't know the details, and probably never would. None of my business. But Mal seemed to take him under his wing, so I always suspected it had to do with drugs.

What I did know was how Smoke looked at me sometimes, like he wanted to lick me from head to toe. Even the way his fiery gaze had drifted straight over to me now. Hell. I forced my brain to think of something else—like a nest of hornets stinging my dick in order to keep the hardness from swelling my pants right in front of the damn club president.

I had never tried coming on to him, and he returned the favor. But if looks could kill, we'd have incinerated each other across the room thousands of times over. That's how I knew he wanted me but was toeing the line, same as me.

"What's up, Prez?" Smoke pulled up a stool. Jonas, who was constantly pushing those reddish-brown strands behind his ears, made room for one more at the bar.

How's the new recruit working out?" Mal asked. "Still out on patrol?"

"Yeah, I left him with Felix," Smoke said, retrieving a pack of gum from his back pocket. It was a habit I'd come to associate him with. Which explained his spicy cinnamon scent.

Mal spun his empty shot glass in his fingers. "Any problems tonight?"

"Nah, been quiet." I felt Smoke's gaze on me as I reached for the empty keg beneath the tap.

"Got a new assignment for you," Mal said, tilting his head to the Scorpions member sitting beside him. "Think you're ready to play with the big boys?"

Smoke's eyebrow quirked up. "You mean I haven't been already?"

He didn't give away smiles very easily, so when the corner of his lip tilted like that, it definitely left my tongue wagging.

Mal and Fish exchanged smirks and knowing glances.

"Of course I'm ready," Smoke said with certainty in his voice.

That was the thing about Smoke. He had a quiet confidence about him. Like smooth velvet over solid muscles. And hell, if that wasn't attractive about the guy, I didn't know what was.

"You'd have a vested interest in this one," Mal said, and a tempered look passed between them that told me it had to do with Smoke's past. He'd come to the Disciples from the Devil's Asylum, one of the most ruthless motorcycle clubs in the Midwest.

I didn't want to seem overly interested, so I left the relatively empty bar to deposit the keg in the storage room before heading back their way to grab a fresh towel and wipe my hands. The after work crowd would be filing in soon, so I made sure the pretzel bowls were full as well.

"Fish has been having some trouble, so he needs your help, if you know what I mean," I heard Mal say. In club speak that meant that Mal needed Smoke to use his former contacts to help the Scorpions out.

"Got it, Prez."

I kept my head averted to attend to my task of mopping up a large wet spot on the bar. But for some reason, a shiver stole across my shoulders. I didn't know why. I had seen and heard plenty of shit way more dangerous than this.

The door jangled open, and two biker babes walked in wearing outfits that left little to the imagination. Believe it or not, I preferred my women more conservative. If they didn't don a short skirt or spiked heels, they garnered my attention every single time.

Several guys in the club were all about getting some action, but to me, these two looked like used up Barbie dolls. And the guys who regularly slept with them? The ultimate man whores. I pretended Smoke wasn't in that same category, even though I'd seen him flirt with his share of ladies.

It made me damn curious how else he spent his time.

The two regulars, one blonde and one brunette, sidled up to the bar, where the brunette ordered a margarita on the rocks, no salt. "Hey, Vaughn," the brunette said in a flirty voice.

"Hey yourself," I said, reaching for the triple sec. I ignored how she leaned over, showing off her cleavage. When I turned back, she was still propped over the bar, and I allowed my eyes to linger even though it didn't do much for me.

"What can I get you, darling?" My gaze slid over her shoulder to her blonde friend and instead met stunning green eyes. Smoke could disarm me with one lustful glance. Sure, the guys might've thought he was salivating over these women, but I knew better. He'd been teasing me mercilessly for months with those meaningful looks that told me he wanted to screw my brains out. And the fucker knew exactly what he was doing to me as his gaze shot down to my fast filling boner.

"A hard cider," the blonde girl said as her friend stayed in the same position with her tits hanging out. I grabbed the bottle of cider and slid it past the brunette, whose gaze was focused on the television above my head.

The blonde grabbed the bottle and turned to Smoke as my jaw tensed. It wasn't like I hadn't witnessed this scenario before. Smoke played the part and enjoyed it as much as I did. As was evidenced now when he slid his arm around her shoulder. Though his eyes were still pinned to mine.

"Want to go somewhere private?" I heard her rasp. His ruddy lips, almost in the shape of a heart, moved to her ear to whisper something more than likely dirty, his gaze never retreating from mine. So as not to call suspicion to myself, I reached for a dirty glass to tuck beneath the bar.

But hell, just waiting for his response made my dick tent my pants. I needed to keep my eyes averted or I was likely to come right then and there.

And now my imagination would run hog wild tonight beneath my sheets. I probably needed a hookup with somebody just to get him out of my head.

"Might happen," Smoke said in that level and self-assured voice. And then his fingers grazed his zipper. "Getting nice and hard thinking about it."

Hot holy damn, I almost combusted right then and there. I felt my neck and cheeks fire right up like a torch. Why in the hell he teased me so ruthlessly, I didn't know.

Right then Mal stepped toward the middle of the bar. "I need to wrap up some business on this end, ladies."

"Sure thing, Mal," the brunette said and headed toward the unoccupied pool table, Jude and Cory long gone.

I moved down the bar to check on my other customers, because I couldn't even look Smoke in the eye without wanting to jump over the bar and tackle him onto the floor. Also because, even though Mal didn't hide most conversations from me, I wasn't going to act like I could listen to club business freely.

Besides, it was hard for me to stay sedentary in my own bar. There was always something that needed to be done, and I liked keeping my hands moving.

"Vaughn," Mal said, halting me in my tracks. "What happened to your part-timer?"

"Joe?" I asked, keeping my gaze focused on Mal. "Doing time on an assault charge from some neighbor dispute. Supposed to get a reduced sentence but still not sure when he'll be out."

"Sounds like you're shorthanded."

"I'll manage." Joe helped tend bar three nights a week. It was hard to find somebody trustworthy who would be willing to keep his or her trap shut. Joe had enough of his own troubles to be really concerned with club business. He rarely interacted with anybody, but I could count on him to get the job done.

Mal thumped Smoke on the back. "Why don't you give our friend here a hand for a while?"

My eyebrows rose and my lips felt cemented together. I could hear the thump, thump, thump of my heart.

"You used to tend bar at your family's business, right?"

"Uh, sure," Smoke struggled to get out. "But I…"

"You could split time between here and the auto shop," Mal said, his forearms flexing on the bar top. "I'll move you off regular patrols since I need you for that other club business."

Still I stood there and gaped at Mal.

"You cool with that?" Mal asked, waiting for me to say something. Anything. "Smoke's a hard worker. Loyal. Trustworthy."

Finally I got my body unstuck. Along with my mouth.

"Don't have to convince me." I shrugged. "You say he's good for it, then he is. Would help me out until Joe is released."

Smoke's head was angled toward the back of the room, looking at the ladies racking up the balls at the pool table. As if he couldn't possibly maintain eye contact with me, either.

"Why don't you…uh," I said, trying to form some semblance of a sentence. "Stop by tomorrow afternoon so I can bring you on board."

He turned at the sound of my voice and stared hard at me. "Yeah, sure."

Mal nodded as if dismissing the conversation, so I moved down the bar, trying not to stumble over my own two wobbly boots. For months on end, I saw Smoke only in passing in my bar, and now I'd be stuck working with him. Fuck.

After a few minutes of shooting the breeze with the regulars at the other end, I moved back down the bar to reach for the remote and change the channel to a different game.

"I need you to be my go-to guy on this operation. You cool with that?" I heard Mal ask Smoke.

"Yeah, Prez," he said. "What's it about?"

Mal turned to Fish and tipped his chin, silently giving him the go-ahead to explain the details.

"We need you to share some intel on the Asylum," Fish said. "Word is they're casing the Russians goods, and we're trying to make it right."

"No problem," Smoke said, though from studying his features dozens of times across the room, I could see a split second of trepidation in his gaze.

And that surprised me because Smoke—hell, all of these guys—seemed to have nerves of steel. The most I'd ever had to deal with was some punks showing up and kicking them out on their asses.

Or that one time a rival club tried to bring their bad blood into my bar. Guy aimed a knife in my direction, but Mal quickly diffused the situation.

I'd admit I'd grown to admire and probably even care about these guys, so I worried about them. All of them—not only Mal and Smoke.

But fuck. Best never to let that show.

CHAPTER TWO
SMOKE

Mal and Jonas had headed toward the back room to see Fish out, leaving me alone with my thoughts at the bar. Not that there was any other damn place I needed to be right then. Heading back to my place would feel way too quiet; it usually was, at this time of night. Unless Felix was knocking around downstairs or cranking his music loud.

We rented the first and second floors of a house on a fairly quiet street. By this point, the neighbors had gotten used to the sound of our hogs rumbling down the road. Some waved, others kept to themselves, but one thing was for certain—the neighborhood was safer because of us, whether they acknowledged that fact or not. Though some might not even realize that we patrol our own turf and keep the lowlifes to a minimum.

I knocked my knuckles on the wooden edge, trying not to watch Vaughn's ass in that faded denim. If only I hadn't seen his cock. It was standing tall and thick and proud the morning he'd used the shower at the compound. He'd caught me staring and it had only made him harder, and fuck, had we been alone, I'd have been on my knees in an instant.

We'd had a party the night before, and Mal was always razzing Vaughn about never taking time away from the bar. So he'd shocked me by showing up, drinking his fill, and crashing in one of the rooms. Though he hadn't been back since.

As usual, Vaughn was shooting the shit at the other end of the room. "And then my stepmom told me to get my ass inside before she whipped my behind," he said, and the customers laughed. The regulars loved him. And the ladies practically melted into the bar top for him. Though he flirted, I'd never seen him with a steady lady on his arm.

"What a card." Lou was a regular and had stationed himself on a stool next to me. The bar erupted into groans as the hockey game on the screen turned violent. An elbow to the face, blood on the ice, a player evicted. "I had a hundred bucks riding on that one."

I stayed away from any and all forms of gambling. I didn't need another addiction to wreck my life. I thumped his shoulder in sympathy and turned my attention back to the screen, avoiding eye contact with the blonde and the brunette who spotted me solo again at the bar.

Goddamn, what a night of surprises. First I'd been told to pick up the slack here in the Hog's Den with the one man I attempted to show zero emotion toward. Except when I wanted to make him sweat. That was a hell of a lot of fun and nobody ever suspected anything.

Except for Cory and Jude, and that was only because they couldn't not notice shit like that. But they'd never open their mouths about it. I'd come to know them and trust them over the past year.

But the way that man looked at me. Christ. With those malt-liquor-colored eyes. More and more I'd been wondering if we shouldn't just get this thing between us out in the open. Work through it, though obviously not in front of the Disciples. They were an organization that didn't stray far from original club code. Though I'd heard one time that Malachi had considered allowing his old lady into the inner circle.

Until she died of an overdose. Same as Mal's dad, the former president of the Disciples. I knew Mal had a soft spot where addiction was concerned because he allowed me entrance into this club. I saw it in his gaze those times he'd come over to the Asylum's compound—when they'd been on better terms—and I'd been as high as Mount Everest.

He saw something in my eyes, I suppose. Enough to ask if I needed help that one night. And I was vulnerable enough to say yes. He'd stepped in like my savior, had practically saved my life. Gave me the kick in the ass I'd needed, and I could never repay him. Certainly not by letting my queer side show.

Except lately all I'd done is fantasize about Vaughn. About that thick cock and those monster thighs. How smooth his skin looked beneath that black downy hair on his legs, fresh out of the shower.

"Club soda with lime, yeah?" Vaughn materialized in front of me, knowing exactly the thing I was craving. He set the glass down, held my eyes for a second too long, and then turned to the group of patrons who'd just walked inside.

Hell yes, I'd want one night with that guy. One long-ass night, where we got it all out of our system. Still, it could go terribly wrong in one way or another.

And now I was going to be stuck working with him? Fuck. I swallowed down the fizzy beverage, which helped douse that fire burning inside me.

I only hoped that I could remember how to make a damn drink. Should come right back, wasn't rocket science. Might be missing some flare, though. The kind of effortless charisma that Vaughn seemed to possess in droves.

I hadn't tended bar in years, not since my dad's joint burned to the ground with him inside. A ton of crap went down between then and now, and I'd been pumping some heavy shit into my veins on almost a nightly basis.

I'd turned myself completely around since then. I wanted to impress Mal, show him that I no longer needed hard drugs. I had done two stints of rehab for the stuff, the last time being two years ago.

Good thing was, I never had a taste for alcohol, like some guys in my program who'd been saddled with cross addictions—the booze and the crack, the weed and the prescription drugs. Unless cinnamon gum was a thing. Hell, at least it wasn't cigarettes.

Nah, for me, I had gotten my first taste of heroin and was a goner. Even now I could still feel her scorching my veins, making me feel completely invincible. Nothing had ever come close. But she became my fucking nightmare and I had to let her go.

The day I walked out clean, Mal had been there waiting for me, and I had never looked back. This brotherhood was different and I didn't want to ruin a good thing. Even earlier, when Mal asked me to help Fish out with my old club, I couldn't show him how freaked it'd gotten me.

I had seen some of my former brothers in passing over the years, but I was never alone, and Mal had said I was in the free and clear. He'd told my previous prez that the recruit to the Disciples was personal, and my prez let me go. Mal and I had pretended that we had some kind of mutual tie to our pasts, but it wasn't anything more that Mal settling some emotional shit inside himself.

By that time, I'd been such a train wreck and so totally useless to my club that it almost hurt how easily they had let me walk out that door. Still, I was thankful every day that they did, and now I was being dragged back into their business. I'd confess, it unnerved me.

The blonde and the brunette had found their opportunity to return and finish business, except I'd only been pretending to be interested because I wanted to mess with Vaughn. I sure as shit wasn't into these ladies. Not tonight. Problem was that they didn't care whom they hooked up with as long as it was a club member, which made them just as bad as the guys who did them time and again because they'd keep their mouths shut about any cheating.

I'd always told myself that if I ever had an old lady, I'd never betray her trust. But what the hell did I know? I'd never found somebody to call my own and probably never would. These guys viewed sex as messing around and nothing more. Sometimes it wigged me out how they stuck their cocks into any willing girl's pussy.

Was I interested in getting my cock sucked? Sure. And I had done that on several occasions. But lately I wasn't attracted to delicate lips—only firm and manly lips. It'd been way too long. My gaze sought Vaughn's down the bar just as his tongue flicked out to trace his mouth. The fleshy tip passed over a small scar right below the bottom of his pucker and hell if the front of my pants didn't pull tight.

A couple of the recruits swept inside, and I immediately pushed the brunette off on Simon. He might've been new, but could hang with the best of them. She didn't seem to mind either way, and that was my whole damn point.

Still, she reached out her hand to rub along my neck, maybe hoping for a threesome.

"Another time," I said, taking a step back.

When Vaughn's bronzed gaze rose to meet mine, I stared hard before tipping my chin in a silent goodbye. It was bound to be awkward with both of us behind that bar.

CHAPTER THREE
VAUGHN

It was a Thursday and Smoke was due at the bar this afternoon. I tried not giving him one damn thought as I jumped in the shower, but I failed miserably as my hand wound its way around my cock. I figured it wouldn't hurt to release some of this sexual frustration.

After getting dressed, I drove to the grocery store to stock my refrigerator as well as my old man's, whose hip replacement surgery had placed him out of commission. Though by now he was supposed to be out and about more. Instead, the procedure had almost made him sedentary. Which wasn't good for a man with a heart condition. He was supposed to be taking daily walks and keeping his sodium intake low.

I carried the two brown grocery bags inside his house and placed them on his counter. Immediately I heard the pulsing beat of the dozens of clocks Pop has positioned around the house. He and my stepmom, Leanne, had been into antiques big time before her death. They'd spend their weekends at flea markets and estate sales, bringing home all kinds of junk.

Dad had always returned with a clock of some sort, even still wore a Timex on his wrist from his youth. Grandfather clocks, rooster clocks, King Tut clocks. Any kind of strange looking ticker, he'd bargained for. Used to drive me insane, but now it was strangely a comfort. To walk through that door and hear that rhythm that somehow regulated my own heartbeat.

Dad was in his recliner with the television blaring in the other room. "Hey Pop, you okay?"

"Yeah, fine," he said, not even twisting his damn head to greet me. Without even looking, I knew one of two channels was live on his screen. Either the one with the pawn shop episodes or that antiques show. He loved to guess right along with the experts how much value the piece had. He used to own a little shop back in the day, which is where I must've gotten my business sense.

I knew his mobility was limited, but I wished he'd try to get out of the house more often, even if I needed to cart his ass around.

"How long have you been propped in front of that television?"

"Long enough, I suppose," he said, finally muting the show, which showcased some kind of classic printing press, and turned his head toward me. There were smudges beneath his eyes like maybe he hadn't been sleeping so well.

"Want to come up to the bar for dinner tonight, Pop?" I asked, unloading the bread on the counter and the milk in the refrigerator. "Maybe your friend Jim can pick you up. When was the last time you kicked back with a beer?"

He stared at me hard and then sighed. "You're probably right. Maybe I'll give Jim a call."

My dad still didn't own a cell phone even though I'd encouraged him to buy one in the case of an emergency. So I picked up his landline from the end table and handed him the receiver before I returned to putting his fruit and vegetables away.

After he got off the phone he made his way to the kitchen, and I tried not to stare at his painfully slow pace. I wasn't going to baby him. He needed to be exercising that muscle, not sitting in that chair for so damn long.

I motioned to him with an apple before putting the rest in a bowl.

He accepted the Red Delicious, his favorite, taking a hearty bite.

"If you want, we can find a good flea market in driving distance. You haven't bought another clock since Leanne passed."

Sadness filtered through his eyes. Maybe I had hit the nail on the head. Maybe time had all but stopped for him since she died more than six years ago. I felt like shit for even mentioning it.

"Look, Pop. I just worry you ain't—"

"No need to even say it," he said, chewing on his apple. "I'll get back out there when I'm good and ready."

He held my gaze, sturdy as a locomotive, and I knew to drop the subject.

"How's business at the bar lately?" he asked, taking a seat at the kitchen table.

"Pretty decent," I said, noticing how thin he looked as he angled himself in the chair. "Packed on the weekends as usual."

I'd owned the Hog's Den back when my investor—also known as the last guy I had steadily fucked—pulled out, skipped town, and left me with a flailing business. I was simply trying to keep me and my pop afloat after my stepmother had passed away from a long bout of liver cancer. The medical bills were piling up, and he had retired from his factory job to tend to her.

I had gone to high school with a friend of the Disciples named Kurt. Apparently he had spoken to Mal, who approached me at my place of business one day. He asked to invest in the bar and allow it to be a resting spot of sorts for his club. He said he'd front the money for improvements.

I'd been leery at first because the Disciples' reputation had preceded them. We were a family of motorcycle aficionados. My pop and uncle had been with a vintage Harley group at one time that in no way identified with the one-percenters, the ratio of owners who considered themselves outlaws. We just genuinely enjoyed riding.

Mal convinced me he was changing his club's tactics and it might take a couple more years. He had pulled them out of drugs, was working on leaving the gun trade, and assured me that I'd have an out at any time, no questions asked. But he needed a solid place to land with somebody he could trust, and I guess Kurt told him I was good for it.

So with my pop's blessing, I gave it a decent shot. I had no other choices anyway. Turned out we were a fit. I was no saint, that was for certain; I'd had my share of run-ins with the police in my younger, more stupid days. But climbing into your thirties did something to you—made you think about life and where it was heading.

"Didn't you mention that you're out a bartender?" Pop raised an eyebrow like he was gearing up to lecture me. "When are you replacing him? You're going to wear yourself down, son. You work too much."

"You know it's hard to find a good fit with that crowd," I said. "But I got somebody filling in tonight."

Pop knew full well that the Disciples needed to be down with you in order for you to be accepted into any segment of their organization, even if it was only manning a part of their bar.

"That bar is all I got," I said when he crossed his arms. "Just how it is, Pop."

My stepmom was forever asking me about settling down with a nice girl. But how did you tell your folks that you've never even come close to finding the right one, and that all your fantasies lately consisted of one guy with a lean body and a large dick?

"Who is it?" Pop asked suddenly, as if he'd been privy to my fantasies.

"His name is Smoke, one of Mal's boys. Guess he has prior experience or something," I said, ducking my head so he didn't see the wash of color. "I'll find out later."

"What the hell kind of name is that? Them boys and their nicknames," he said, crunching into his apple again. "A good solid name is all you need in this town."

I never considered why I didn't know Smoke's real name or how he'd come to own that moniker. Though I could only imagine.

"Who knows," I said, shutting the refrigerator door. "I'll bet you had yourself a nickname or two back in the day."

A ghost of smile tilted the corner of his lips. No doubt he was remembering his former glory days.

"So what did Jim say?" I angled my head toward the phone. "He picking you up for a burger and beer?"

"Yeah," he said and then pitched the apple core into the garbage can behind him. "So we'll be up around dinner time."

"Good thing, Pop," I said, making my exit. "See you then."

I headed to my place to unload my own groceries. I made myself a turkey sandwich for lunch, and then lifted some free weights to blow off steam or maybe more sexual frustration. Always did lately, especially if there was a good chance that Smoke would show his face in the bar that night. And now I was going to have to actually work with him.

Goddamn. But maybe this was good. Maybe he wouldn't be such a darn enigma anymore once I heard more than a couple strings of sentences out of his mouth.

Thing was, even though we barely spoke more than a few words at a time, we were always on the same wavelength, it seemed. All I needed to do was give him a look and he'd provide backup to kick some douche out or to give me the heads-up that the prez was on his way back to the bar.

It was as if we had some damn mental telepathy or something. Like there were cobwebs of understanding and tension continually linking us together.

Fuck. Here goes.

I grabbed my keys, hopped on my bike, and drove my ass to the bar.

CHAPTER FOUR
SMOKE

I put some hours in that morning at Chrome, the club's auto parts store, and stayed into the afternoon to work on a couple of my metal art pieces. I'd made the signs hanging on the walls in the Hog's Den and a few for the guys' bachelor pads.

It was something I always did to blow off steam—plus, I was decent at it—and I could've used a dose of distraction right about then. No such luck. All I could picture was Vaughn's full mouth with those wine-stained lips, the jagged scar beneath, and his biceps flexing in that damn Hog's Den shirt while his fist pumped me into oblivion.

Still, it felt good to hold those sharp and rough pieces and mold them into whatever I wanted in the back room of the shop. I loved the creative outlet, but I was always so busy, I didn't realize how much I missed it until I got my hands dirty again.

Mal threw a smile my way when he stopped by the store and encouraged me to work more shifts. I was cool with wherever Mal assigned to me because being with his club had given me purpose again. I was so far down the rabbit hole a couple years ago that I thought for sure I was on the road to my death.

If being with the Asylum hadn't killed me, I would have died by my own hands. I was pumped so full of drugs, it was a wonder that my heart beat all on its own. So being able to put my brain and my body to good use had its rewards.

I pulled up to the nearly empty lot of the Hog's Den and parked right next to Vaughn's Harley Roadster. Our bikes were twin versions, black and orange. Fire and smoke. Spark and flame.

This felt like a clandestine meeting, after we'd pretty much avoided direct contact with each other for months. Go figure. I'd only ever seen Vaughn at the bar and rarely at the compound. The man seemed to work nonstop, like he was married to his job. Kinda like all of us were sworn to the club.

Vaughn's back was to me when I stepped through the door. Those damn ragged jeans with those heavy black boots. That white T-shirt with the blue lettering pulling tight across his muscular back.

Right then he turned to me, a stack of pitchers in his arms, and we gazed across the bar at each other.

Finally my legs moved toward him. "Ready to work."

"Yeah?" He struggled not to slide his gaze down the front of me. Tried, but failed. "Sorry if the prez put you in a tough spot."

"Nah, it's a nice change of pace," I said, because it was the truth. "Actually enjoyed working in my bar."

"What bar was that?" he asked, dumping his armload on the bar top.

I straightened one of pitchers nearly spinning off the side. "It was a little place off the interstate called Mitsy's."

"Sounds familiar," Vaughn said, his eyes losing focus as he tried picturing it. It was a small, run-down building with a neon sign, in the middle of nowhere, but it had always felt like a second home. "Wasn't that the place involved in an arson?"

"My family owned it. Thought I'd inherit it some day." My hand gripped the barstool until my fingers turned colorless. "Before everything went to shit."

"That's messed up," he said, storing the pitchers on the lower shelf. "Sorry to hear that."

The story of what happened in that bar one night was too horrible to speak out loud. How my dad was tied up and robbed before the building was set on fire. I had taken off with friends after midnight, and the guilt of not being there was almost too much to bear. The case still remained unsolved.

My father might've made some enemies on the street in his youth because of his involvement in some petty crime. But he had built that bar with his own hands, even furnished our tiny upstairs apartment to his liking, and the neighborhood had accepted us with open arms. Something about how it all went down always niggled in the back of my brain.

When I was with the Asylum club, trashed out of my mind one night, one dude had hinted that our president, Terrence, knew who'd done the dirty deed—but I could've been making that shit up in my own brain. Later, I'd asked one of the guys named Jake, but he had shrugged it off, telling me I'd been hallucinating.

I realized that Vaughn was still staring at me, but he'd never ask me to elaborate. It wasn't his place. That was one of the things I liked about him. He knew never to push too hard.

"First things first. Let me get you a Hog's Den shirt," he said. "Should probably take off your cut while you're working with me."

I nodded and pretended not to stare at his ass as he led me to the small storage room that doubled as Vaughn's office to remove my leather vest. It was next to a larger room where the club met on this turf, and it seemed a shame that he got shafted.

The Disciples owned controlling interest in the bar. But it was Vaughn who did all the work, and that was a hard feat. I remembered how much my dad had put into Mitsy's. The long hours, simply trying to turn a profit. The Hog's Den might as well have belonged to Vaughn.

I wondered if Vaughn ever had those thoughts. About owning something outright, like I did sometimes. Hell, I was lucky to be alive and sober. But sometimes, I wondered how all of my hard work would pay off. Where it would get me besides being part of a brotherhood, which had its own rewards, sure.

At least now I was in it for all the right reasons. Before I was completely lost and merely grateful to have a place to call a temporary home. I'd been manipulated, but I also didn't have big enough balls back then to stand on my own two feet.

I should've kept in touch with my uncle, who owned stake in my father's bar. Instead, I watched numbly as he took off, too shocked and grief-stricken to talk about it any further. I attempted to reach him a couple of times over the years, but he never returned my calls, and eventually he got a new number. Since then, I had plenty of questions about what went down, but I always buried them while I attempted to make something of my life.

Vaughn handed me the neatly folded cotton with the Hog's Den insignia on the back. I took off my cut, and as my fingers reached up to peel my own shirt over my neck, he looked away.

"I'll, uh…" he said, his legs eating the distance toward the door. "I'll leave you to it, then."

"It's only a shirt," I said, surprised at the roughness of my own voice. I had been naked in front of plenty of men and women, and I couldn't handle having my shirt off in front of one dude?

He stood rooted to his spot, scratching his head, and then his eyes darted up to mine. But not before snagging on my stomach and then sliding over my pecs. I knew I had a decent physique, not as muscled as Vaughn; still, I couldn't help feeling somehow singed by his gaze.

I nudged the material over my shoulders. "You act like you've never seen a naked guy's chest before."

"Of course I have," he snapped, and then he held my eyes.

"So what's the problem?" I asked as the shirt descended over my chest and he followed the material with his eyes.

Vaughn said nothing for long moments as we stood staring at each other.

I didn't know what the hell compelled me to do it, but I took a stalking pace nearer. Pure adrenaline, I supposed. Mixed with longing. "Asked you a question."

Stepping backward, his shoulders hit the wall. Our eyes snagged and held. "No problem at all."

"You sure?" I said, swinging my head down and studying his lips. How the slash of plum color was a direct contrast to that white mark beneath. My dick was painfully hard against my zipper and I resisted adjusting myself. "Maybe I don't believe you."

"No?" he said in the meekest voice as his tongue swiped over his bottom lip, always slicking across that scar, as if soothing what was likely a childhood souvenir.

A noise from the other room caused both of us to tense. It was a couple of the Disciples entering through the back door, and we could hear their dulled conversation through the wall.

"Fuck," I said, unwilling to draw my eyes or my body away from his. "You plan on making this difficult?"

His gaze swung down to my unflagging erection. "Maybe."

"They can't know," I muttered as if he hadn't already deduced that himself. He didn't seem shocked or even resistant to my statement. As if we were finally acknowledging it. The elephant in the room. Our heart-pounding, searing attraction to each other.

"No shit," he grunted before he drew even closer. His breaths released in heavy gusts. Fuck, I wanted to eat his lips, swipe my tongue across that ridged scar, and drive my knee between his legs to feel his length.

My palm landed on the wall beside him. "How many guys you been with?"

"Enough," he said as I caged him in. "You?"

I huffed out a breath. "Same."

It was like we were speaking our own language. We'd both been around the block enough times to know what we wanted.

"Vaughn," the vice president, Jonas, barked from the hallway.

"In here," Vaughn said as he stepped around me to open the door. As he did so, his lips drew dangerously close to my face. His eyes remained planted on my mine as our mouths practically brushed.

One last glance, his gaze fueled with molten heat. I nearly melted to the ground in a pile of my own come.

Chapter Five
Vaughn

Man, we were only playing with fire. That was the closest I'd ever gotten to Smoke. When he backed me against that door, his hot breath fanned across my lips with the spice of cinnamon gum, and I could feel the heat from his warm skin. My heart played a crazy rendition of its own. Thump, thump, thump.

"What's up?' I asked Jonas, trying to clear my throat. "Just getting Smoke set up."

"We need to keep the back area clear for some visitors arriving tonight."

"Visitors?" Smoke surfaced, adjusting his bar T-shirt and tucking it down into his pants.

To anybody else right then, it might've looked like we'd been getting it on. But these guys, the Disciples, would never even give it a second thought. Two men together was probably the furthest thing from their minds.

"A few top-level Scorpions, remember?" Jonas said, pushing aside his long bangs. "Just hanging out, celebrating a couple of things."

Without saying another word, I knew he was referring to the takedown of a drug cartel that had stolen from the Scorpions. Jude and Cory had been involved with the whole mess, along with the feds, but it had all worked out in the end.

"Right," Smoke said. "Except this time I'll be helping behind the bar."

Jonas smirked. "I'm sure Vaughn could spare you for a few minutes to come say hello to the guys."

"Of course," I said, clapping Jonas on the back. "I'll rope off that back corner for you."

Sliding behind the bar, I finished slicing some lemons and limes that I had found in the back cooler, on the verge of losing their color. It was bound to get busy during the dinner rush, and the more preliminary effort I put in, the more sales I made on quickly prepared drinks.

I saw that Lewis, my cook, was already an elbow deep in his own prep work. Our bar menu was small—we kept it that way on purpose—but Lewis's wings were a favorite in this town.

I used to snack on them a couple of times a week, which had become a nasty habit. No way I wanted to be walking around with a beer belly. Which is why I also laid off the beer. Keeping fit was important to me, not only because I had to remain on my toes behind this bar, but also with a family history of heart disease.

I got busy stacking enough beer glasses down below for the draft drinkers who comprised the majority of our customers. We also supplied a couple of popular native brews that kept the locals coming back.

I felt Smoke's heat before he even spoke a word. "Okay, Boss, what do I need to know?"

A smile tilted my lips. "*Boss*, is it?"

"Whatever," he mumbled, his cheeks staining a darker pink, matching the precise color of his lips.

I liked throwing Smoke off balance. He always seemed so unruffled and composed. Except for that last five minutes in the back room. "Just the usual. Joe doubled as my bar back on busy nights. We got it all done with good teamwork. So keep an eye out to be sure beer, glasses, fruit, juices, and ice are well stocked."

His gaze traveled the length of the bar, taking note of the beverage well and service station. "Got it."

"You remember how to make your drinks?"

"Probably all the typical ones," he said, checking the back shelf of liquor. "Pretty sure no one who steps in here orders one of them fancy cosmopolitans."

I nearly argued his point, but he was mostly right. We served the usual blue-collar fare; this was no trendy bar, for sure.

"Right," I conceded. "But plenty of gin and tonics, black and tans, that kind of thing."

"Easy enough," he said, chomping his gum while he eyed the drafts on tap.

I placed the extra limes in a Tupperware container below the bar. "Then I'm sure you're all set."

"If I have trouble remembering, I'll ask," he said. "And I'll be sure to stay out of your way. My dad always complained about open ice hits."

I laughed at his hockey reference and figured I'd probably like his father. He smiled to himself almost wistfully, as if remembering a decent time in his life, and something tugged at my gut.

Smoke definitely understood proper bar etiquette. Assistants knew to give the head bartender a wide berth. They helped out however they could, especially with keeping supplies properly stocked, and never got in the way of a direct sale with the customer.

"Just help me figure out the cash drawer?"

I dipped my head and walked to the register. He stood back and looked over my shoulder, but I could still feel his breath on my neck. If he stepped one foot closer, I might even feel his package right against my ass. I took a deep breath and pressed the key to open the drawer. But damn, the man smelled like cinnamon and sweat, and I wanted to lick the briny taste straight off his cock.

I showed him what buttons to punch for certain drinks. "Pretty straightforward. You run into a problem, just give a holler. And no substitutions on the menu."

"What is this button for?" His hand reached over my shoulder, which briefly placed his chest flush against my back, and I was sure he could hear my intake of breath.

He inched away. "Fuck."

I pretended like nothing at all had happened. Too bad I could feel how his cock stiffened instantly behind his zipper before he pulled way. This was going to be one hell of a long night. "Use that button to void any food or drink orders and then start from scratch."

"Got it," he said in a rough voice.

"Hey, Vaughn." As the door swung open, my server stepped inside. Besides Lewis, she was my only full-time staff and was a godsend on my busiest nights. I used two other part-timers to help out during the week. They were all cool chicks, a bit rough around the edges, which was necessary in this establishment—but they worked hard and brought in good tips.

"Hey Cherry," I said, crooking my neck toward her. "Smoke's going to be helping out on busy nights until we find a replacement for Joe."

She didn't even bat an eyelash. Never did with any bar or club matters. She flirted a bit with the customers for larger tips, but she had an old man back home whom she was loyal to. She was a perfect employee to have. No drama. No questions. Besides, she knew better. She'd be out fast on her ass if she tried to dig around in anybody's business.

Customers began straggling through the door, the blue-collar after-work crowd. I looked over at Smoke, who seemed to have pulled himself back together. He was staring at the bottles of vodka as if memorizing them. "We don't carry any of the fruity kind, in case somebody asks."

He arched his eyebrow and smirked. "Fruity kind?"

"Yeah, you know, blueberry, vanilla…none of that shit."

"Didn't even know there were so many types," he said. "Mitsy's never carried that stuff, either. Been a while since I tended bar, I guess."

"Hey, listen, handle these customers walking in," I said, nodding toward the foursome wearing construction crew gear. I lifted my hand in a wave. They'd been in here a few times before. "Get your feet wet before we're balls to the wall in here. Though that usually only happens on weekends."

He nodded. "Sounds like a plan."

Off he went to ask the guys down the bar for their order. Before I knew it he was filling up drafts expertly, with little foam off the top. Came back to him real quick. He looked like a natural, too, and I had to wonder if he ever missed it.

Though he was probably barely legal when he helped out his dad. I steered clear of mentioning anything more about those rumors of his father dying in that fire, and his uncle moving out of town pronto, which meant Smoke had lost his family. Damn. He must've had a shit decade of his life, but hopefully his childhood had been happier.

Right then my pop and his friend walked through the door, and I felt grateful that he was still alive and kicking. If only he'd taken better care of himself. I wished Leanne were still around to keep him in line. Even her grown children from a previous marriage hadn't visited in a while. I made a mental note to give my stepsiblings a call and invite them into town over the next holiday weekend.

"Good to see you." Cherry made a beeline for my dad and kissed him on the cheek. "Got your favorite table reserved just for you."

"Sounds good, honey," he said and then lifted his eyes to me.

"Hey, Pop, I'll be over in a bit," I said and then greeted his friend with a wave.

Suddenly Smoke was standing right beside me. "Your old man?"

"Yeah, just had a hip replacement," I said as I watched Cherry seat them in an empty center booth. "Encouraged him to get out more, especially since his ticker ain't doing so well, either. He comes up from time to time when he's not watching those antiques and pawn shop shows at all hours of the night."

He leaned over the bar. "Huh, guess I never noticed him in here before."

"Probably because you're usually never here long enough to have a seat."

"True. Feels nice to stay put for awhile." His jaw chomped a couple of times on his gum before a dimple indented his cheek. "Outside of running up and down the length of this bar."

The guys at the end of the bar howled with laughter over something and high-fived, while a party of three walked through the door and found a table.

"Well, you know what I mean," Smoke said.

"You mean not living like a nomad out on the road?" I asked, bumping elbows with him.

"Something like that," he said. "Though I'd probably go stir-crazy being cooped up, as well."

"That how you felt working at Mitsy's?"

He took his time thinking about it, and something like nostalgia warmed his gaze. "Guess I don't really know. I was only a kid back then."

"Yeah, I hear you. When you finally reach adulthood," I said, thinking about how wild I'd been in my younger days, "you still don't know your ass from a hole in the wall."

He nodded. "You ever get out of here and do something fun?"

"Depends what you consider fun."

He smirked. "At least I get to ride around. You're stuck inside all night. Though it would be nice to have something solid to be proud of."

"Good thing I enjoy it." I jerked my shoulder. "Let's see…I like listening to good music—real rock music from the 70s, not that pop shit that began in the 80s. Fuck, I feel like I'm reciting one of those dating site applications."

He laughed. "Nice to get to know you better, at least."

I wasn't even sure what more to tell him about myself. My life was so tied to this place. Maybe I did need to get out more.

"Well, turnabout is fair play," I said, feeling something warm slide around my chest. "I'll be sure to drill you later. Gonna say hello to my pop. You got the bar for a few minutes?"

"Yeah, of course." He flicked the towel at my shoulder. "All set."

I walked over to greet my dad and his friend.

"That your new hire?" my father asked.

I almost snorted at that term, because it wasn't like I was paying Smoke. He was on the club's payroll, and they divided their money as they saw fit. But to simplify it for Pop, I nodded.

When I looked over my shoulder, I saw that Smoke was watching us. Did he want to meet my father or something? Or maybe he was only thinking about our conversation. Going with the former, I tilted my head, beckoning him forward.

He looked down the bar as if making sure he was free for a minute and then walked over.

"This is my father," I said to him. "Dad, meet Smoke. He's the guy who made some of these pieces hanging on the wall, from old and new auto parts."

"Is that right?" My dad put his hand out for Smoke to shake. "I like the idea of that. I'm into vintage collectables myself. Where'd you learn to do that, from your old man?"

"Shop class," he said, surprising me. "In high school. Just put something together one day. Teacher let me stay after and use the soldering machine. Said I had something good going and encouraged me to do more."

I was rapt by his story, imagining a younger version of him. He nodded to the piece on the wall behind him. "That there is a lot like the one I made for my family's bar."

He was interrupted by Cherry reaching over to hand Pop and Jim their basket of wings.

"I better head back," Smoke said, looking up at the bar. "It was good to meet you."

"You, too," my dad said. "What the hell kind of name is Smoke, anyway? You got a real one, son?"

I bit my cheek to stop laughing while Smoke nearly cringed. I knew my dad wouldn't be able to hold back asking that question. His friend just smiled and shook his head.

Smoke cleared his throat and looked directly at my pop. "The name is Reed, sir."

Whoa, that totally threw me for a loop. First, I didn't expect Smoke to actually fess up to my dad, and second, I didn't expect his name to be something so…hot.

Reed. Fuck.

He refused eye contact with me as he made his way back to the bar.

I was completely distracted for the next two minutes, imagining how it would sound calling out his name in the heat of passion. I could barely even remember anything my dad's friend had said to me after that.

I quickly bussed a table before filling drink orders for a couple of waiting customers, his real name still on the tip of my tongue.

As Smoke passed by me at the tap, his hip connected with mine. "Don't even fucking think about calling me that," he muttered real low in my ear.

I couldn't help the smirk that tugged at my lips.

Then I heard Cherry's voice ring out from the corner booth. "Better watch yourself."

It was the same two guys who had shown up the hour before and ordered a couple of pitchers of draft. Given the stitched names on their blue uniform shirts and grease-stained fingernails, they looked to be a couple of mechanics blowing off steam after work.

"I meant no harm, darling," the larger guy drawled and reached for Cherry again. She smacked his hand away before it landed point-blank on her ass.

"Do that again and I'll cut off your damn fingers and feed them to you with that hot sauce," Cherry said as I made my way closer. I took stock of their table, which was littered with four empty pitchers and a basket of chicken wings.

Normally Cherry could handle herself, and our regulars knew never to put hands on our servers, but this guy looked about a beer away from falling out of his booth.

Instead of addressing the guy, I decided to deal with his friend instead. "Maybe it's time to take your party elsewhere?"

"Whaddaya mean?" drunk guy said. "We're just relaxing and having a good time."

"I don't call harassing my server—or any woman for that matter—a good time," I said, crossing my arms. "She wanted your hands all over her, she'd ask. But I'm going to guess her old man wouldn't like it one bit. And neither would I."

I only hoped this situation was resolved under the radar before my pop got all out of sorts about the kind of *riffraff* that frequented my bar. That's all I needed to hear about the entire next week. I swear sometimes he liked to ignore the fact that my bar was Disciples turf.

Just then, Jonas walked out of the back room with a couple of Scorpions and zeroed in on our conversation. "You need a hand over there, Vaughn?"

I looked back at Smoke, who stood with his arms splayed on the bar top. Eyes on me, he rolled his shoulder, letting me know he had my back.

"Nope," I said to Jonas. "We're good. Go enjoy yourselves."

The mechanic friend got smart as he eyed the Disciples and Scorpions cuts and stood up, yanking his coworker from the booth. "Let's get the hell out of here."

Jonas still watched them from the back table. "I better not see your faces in this bar again."

CHAPTER SIX
SMOKE

The first week with Vaughn went off without a hitch. I did my time at the auto parts store, talked club business with the Scorpions, and then assisted Vaughn at the Hog's Den on a couple of busy nights.

I could tell Vaughn was grateful to have the help—he seemed even more animated than usual, busting chops and telling stories about his childhood.

"And then my friend Z was like, hell no, I didn't spray paint the side of that bridge," Vaughn was telling some regulars at the bar. I just shook my head and reached around him to get the vodka. But he knew I was there. I heard the hitch in his voice. "J...just ask my pop next time he's in here. He'll tell you how long it took us to clean that sucker off."

And boy, did the ladies love him. Just like I ruthlessly teased him with the brunette the other night, he did the same to me now, leaning over the bar with his meaty forearms, his ass looking perfect in those worn-in jeans, the woman in front of him biting her lip and making eyes. Fuck, this man was going to send me to blue ball hell.

In months past, I could simply walk out the door and head out on patrol, but now I was practically chained to this bar and forced to watch him work the room. Maybe we needed to establish some rules. Maybe that was the only way to get through this without fucking each other's brains out.

Though if I'd had my way the other night, I would've had him flat against the wall, my dick up his ass. But since then, the only thing we did was look, neither one of us broaching the topic again. Maybe both realizing how darn uncomfortable it might be right now if something had happened between us.

If he agreed not to flaunt anything in my face, I'd do the same. As soon as this damn place shut down for the night, I was going to actually bring it up instead of taking off right away like I always did. We were going to have a talk. And then I was getting the hell out of Dodge.

As the night wound down and he kept up his flirting ways, I actually second-guessed myself and wondered if he was actually going to leave with the striking redhead who'd hung out near the bar all night. Hell, maybe he only wanted to get laid. Maybe all of that *hadn't* been for my benefit.

There was only one way to find out. So when the customers began dropping off one by one, and Vaughn signaled that it was closing time, I took the opportunity.

"I'm all set here, if you want to take off," he said while wiping down the bar.

"I was actually going to offer to close up shop if you want to hook up with somebody."

I nodded toward the female eyeing him as she now slowly made her way toward the exit. All he needed to do was say the word and she'd go home with him in an instant.

His eyebrows shot up. "What the hell are you talking about?"

I couldn't help my frustration from seeping through. "The way you were practically humping the bar earlier, I figured you needed to get your rocks off."

Vaughn waved as she went out the door, the disappointment clear on her face.

"Jealous or something?" he asked, tightening his gaze on me.

I swallowed the boulder in my throat. "Figured maybe it'd been a while since you got laid."

"Fuck," he said, practically growling. "For the record, I don't go home with customers. Ever. Especially regulars."

"Why not?" I asked, watching Cherry walk out the door with her large bag and an armful of takeout.

"Believe me, I've learned my lesson," he said. "It can get pretty awkward in here. I take my personal business elsewhere."

I looked around the space, making sure it was empty. Lewis had left an hour ago, since the kitchen had stopped serving food at ten. "Yeah, like where?"

He didn't look me in the eye. "Other bars."

"What other bars?" I knew I was pushing him but hell, I was on edge, ready to combust.

He took a menacing step toward me, invading my space. "What kind of answer you looking for?"

"No answer," I said, realizing I had taken it too far. Vaughn's business was his own. He was making that clear. "Fuck, just forget it. I'm out of here."

I grabbed hold of my keys and tried not to slam my way out the door. I didn't know why the hell I was so rattled by him tonight. I mean, I had been every night, but something about the idea of him being with somebody else right in front of my eyes made me crazy with need. Need that it felt like only he could fulfill.

As soon as I got to my bike, I realized I'd left my cut in the break room. I stood outside, attempting to rein in my uneven pulse. I didn't know what the fuck had come over me.

Breathing more steadily, I stepped back through the door, only to find the bar empty. I'd just grab my leather vest and leave him in peace.

"I forgot my…" I stopped in my tracks because Vaughn stood motionless in the middle of the floor, veins bulging in his neck, as if he'd implode at the slightest touch.

He was always moving and talking with a restless energy in this bar, so his stillness was a bit startling.

"Hey." I gingerly placed my hand on his shoulder. "I'm sorry if I—"

There was instant recoil, as if he were attempting to contain the vortex of tension between us by vacuuming it in through his skin.

He twisted toward me, his eyes latching onto mine, right before I was slammed against the door.

The wind was practically knocked out of me as Vaughn sank his weight against my smaller frame. We were groin to groin, heartbeat to heartbeat.

"Fuck, Vaughn, you're—" Heaving breaths surged through my nostrils. "I was going to suggest a truce."

"Yeah?" he mumbled, his gaze fastening on my mouth. "What sort of truce?"

"You don't flirt with any customers for my benefit…" I gasped as his hip adjusted over mine. "And I'll provide the same courtesy."

His eyes narrowed. "What the hell do you think that's going to accomplish?"

"Maybe we wouldn't get so damn keyed up every time we're in the same room."

"You really think that's going to help?" he spit out.

A strangled grunt ripped from my throat as his cock twitched against mine. I could feel the entire length of him, and damn, did he feel good. I could almost picture that pink head, the long vein running up the front. The way it angled to the side and sat against his firm abdomen.

He spoke against my ear, and a line of electricity buzzed over the hairs on my arms. "You don't think the reason I'm so damn wound up every night is that you're sexy as fuck and I'm desperate to have you?"

"Ah, hell," I rasped out as his fingers braced the back of my neck.

His lips slid hazardously closer to mine. "I think the only thing that's going to solve this problem is getting it over with."

"Getting what—"

And then his mouth came down on mine, tapping all the goddamn air out of my lungs. His lips were surprising soft and hungrily persistent as his tongue forced my lips apart. It'd been so damn long since I'd kissed a man that I was completely taken by his musky scent, the rough stubble on his chin, the raspy grunts releasing from his throat.

Fuck, how I'd missed this. It was just different—even better, depending on the circumstances—being with another dude. And damn, this was Vaughn, the guy I'd fantasized about on more than one occasion.

The kiss was deep and intense, both of us moaning into each other's mouths, his body practically molded to mine, our dicks bumping up against each other.

"Fuck," I said, dragging my mouth away. "Couldn't you have been a shitty kisser or something?"

Vaughn took a step back, but I didn't want him to move away. Not after I'd finally gotten a taste of him. My senses were on overload, and all of my nerve endings were raw and alive and pulsing.

My fingers gripped his nape, and I yanked him toward me to renew our connection.

"What the hell are we doing?" Vaughn asked. Our foreheads rested together.

"I don't know," I said and then swiped my tongue across his plump bottom lip, delving even lower to brush across that scar. "But you started it."

He groaned as his rough fingers grasped at my face. His lips slammed over mine, pressing hard. My tongue darted out to skim against his and then slipped deeply inside his mouth.

This kiss was slower, hotter even, and my head was dizzy with lust. My limbs felt heavy, achy with need. I wanted to strip him down and take him in my mouth right then and there.

Vaughn ground his hips into mine, and his fingers slipped down my back to grip my ass. Our tongued battled for dominance as his lips bruised mine. In another minute, I'd be on my knees, worshipping his fucking cock.

As I pulled him more firmly against me, my phone buzzed in my pocket. I was supposed to call Jonas before my shift to discuss my meeting with the Scorpions, but all thoughts had flitted out of my head as soon as I was in Vaughn's orbit.

Shit. The call was like a slap of reality.

"Damn," I said as my phone buzzed again and Vaughn backed away, breathing heavily. "I gotta take this."

He nodded, raking his fingers through his hair, not meeting my eyes. I made the motion to reach for him but then decided against it. I needed time to think, and so did he.

"Jonas. Sorry man," I said and then slipped out the door.

Chapter Seven
Vaughn

Hot damn. A kiss between us had actually happened and was even better than the fantasy. Smoke's hard body, his smooth and pliant lips. He had gotten me so cranked up tonight slipping behind me at the bar while I flirted shamelessly with the customers. Then he had called me on it, and my need had escalated to a fever pitch.

If his cell hadn't rung, how far would we have taken it?

And now what in the hell did we do?

Maybe if we had one night, swore each other to secrecy, we'd be done with it, and all of this tension could finally end. He'd have to come to my place because he lived above Felix in a double house that they shared.

But Felix and the other recruits also patrolled in my neighborhood. Shit. This was a doomed situation. If only I could get him out of my brain. No chance of that tonight.

I probably needed to go up to Racer's and get my rocks off with some hot guy. Instead, I went home and jacked off to thoughts of Smoke fucking me. Hell, I didn't even know if he was a top or a bottom, but I'd take him any way I could get him.

But rubbing one out only took the edge off, so when I awoke in the morning and realized he'd be on schedule with me again that night, I was strung so damn tight I had to take care of myself again in the shower.

When I got to the Hog's Den that afternoon, I began counting stock immediately, glad for the first time that I didn't have a bar back. Busy work was a bonus right in that moment.

Lewis was already in the kitchen making his wing sauce, but with his headphones on, he was oblivious to the outside world.

We were low on glasses, so I ran them through the washer myself and then began dusting a couple of the shelves behind the bar that held vintage glass steins, even though Mal had set us up with a weekly cleaning service.

I was so lost in thought that my head jerked up when I heard the prez call my name. I was bent over the back display case and almost knocked my skull on the wooden edge.

"What's up, Mal?"

My voice sounded strange. I hoped he couldn't tell I'd been thinking about Smoke and me making out like fucking horny teenagers.

"Hey, listen," he said, clearing his throat. "It's about Smoke."

Panic crowded the back of my throat, cutting off my air supply, as I dreaded what would come out of his mouth next. It was ridiculous to think he suspected anything. Smoke and I had hidden our attraction so well, even he and I hadn't been sure about it until more recently.

"What about him? You need to take him off this job?" I asked, rambling on, attempting to fill up the awkward silence. "I'm sure Joe will be out of the slammer soon and back to work. Guess he had a prior that added time to his sentence. I can manage without him for now."

At least that might relieve the tension as well as our proximity to each other. Though the thought also made me feel strangely bummed because if I admitted it, I liked having Smoke around. He was easy to get along with and was definitely not high maintenance. He came ready to work and never made a fuss about anything. I think he liked being back in this atmosphere, as well.

"No, nothing like that," Mal said, and that prickly feeling eased in my chest. "I only…want you to look out for him, that's all."

I laid down the rag and turned to give him my full attention. "I'm not sure what you mean…"

"It's just…Smoke has had a rough couple of years and now…now he's kind of being pulled back into something I'm not sure he's ready for," Mal said, shadows lining his eyes. "Maybe I shouldn't have assumed…"

"The thing with the other club?"

"Yeah. I'm not sure if it'll stir up too many…. God, I don't know." He rushed his fingers through his hair, almost like a nervous family member. I rarely saw him like this. "Smoke's history is his to tell, so I won't say too much. But he's a good guy, and I'm sorta concerned about him."

"You have a soft spot for him, yeah?" *I do too*, I wanted to say.

"He reminds me too much of something from my own past, and I just want him to come out the other end okay. You feel me?"

"Got it. No problem, Mal."

Fuck, now I felt even more responsible for my actions somehow, even though Smoke and I were two consenting adults.

What the hell *was* Smoke's story?

"Hey, Mal?" I said before I lost the opportunity or my nerve. "I remember that fire. Mitsy's bar? Did the police ever find anything?"

He shook his head. "I've inquired over the years. Even put out feelers to find out where his uncle had disappeared to. Figured Smoke could use some links from his childhood."

"Nothing?"

"Nothing," he said. "At least, not yet. Selfish bastard."

I recognized the frustration in Mal's eyes. He thought Smoke had been dealt a shitty hand. I couldn't agree more.

After Mal left, I was thinking so hard about everything he'd said that when Smoke strode in for his shift, I nearly dropped the bottle of tequila I was replacing on the back shelf. Man, I'd been on edge all day. I needed to pull my head out of my ass.

I could barely look at him without my cheeks heating up. He was wearing those fucking tight jeans with those black laced-up boots. And the way his blond hair curled atop the bandana he wore made me want to shove my fingers beneath it and feel the softness against my rough hands. Given his poor eye contact, I wondered if he had misgivings about what had happened between us last night. Fuck.

Or maybe it was all the tension in the air, choking him in precisely the same way it was choking me.

He tugged the headscarf from his head. He wore it only when he rode. His curls bounced against his forehead. Damn, he was sexy. "Hey, Vaughn. Anything you need besides the usual?"

"Ain't that a loaded question," I said, and something shuttered in his expression. I immediately backpedaled. "Look, about yesterday…"

"It's all cool," he said, cutting off my thoughts. "If you have regrets about what went down…"

"Regrets?" I asked incredulously. My defenses shifted to stand-down position. "Did you not feel my raging hard-on stroking against your groin?"

Smoke momentarily shut his eyes. His hands bunched into fists as if to get a hold of himself. His eyelashes were like golden wings that cast faint shadows on his cheekbones.

"Fuck, say something, Smoke. Because believe me, I liked what happened last night. I just don't know what to do about it."

"Same here." He scrubbed his hand over his face. "Maybe we…I…."

"What?" I said, needing something to do with my hands. I reached for the jar of maraschino cherries I had brought from the back room. "Just say it, man."

"Maybe we need to get it out of our system or whatever," he said, eyes uncertain, voice throaty. "Then some of this—whatever the hell this is between us—can be relieved."

My cock jerked in my pants. I looked around the bar to be certain we were still alone in here. I could hear Lewis banging around in the kitchen. Smoke seemed to be holding his breath as he waited on me.

"Yeah?" I said, taking a step toward him, and I heard a low growl. "One good hard fuck?"

"Something like that," he said, and then his eyes darted to my now raging hard-on.

My fingers locked on the bar top. "Hell, if this wasn't the start of our shift, I'd say let's get it over with now."

"I'd be on board with that," he said, quirking one eyebrow and adjusting the substantial bulge in his own pants. He was as turned on as I was.

He grabbed the jar from me and popped open the lid as my gaze travelled appreciatively over his body. "You a top or a bottom?" I asked.

A dark look crossed over his features. "A top, man. Always a top. You got a problem with that?"

Damn, there was definitely a story there somewhere.

"No problem here," I said, shrugging. "I would never complain about getting it on with someone as hot as you."

Right then a regular came trudging through the door on the heels of Cherry. "Hey, boys."

We both blew out a breath and took a step away from each other, as if we'd been caught screwing on the bar or something. As Smoke moved past me to the service station, his fingers brushed against mine and lingered. It felt like a swarm of fireflies was crammed inside my chest, humming and buzzing and trying to burst free.

The customer sat at the other end, and Smoke served him a draft. When he headed back my way and mumbled, "Tonight," I nearly fucking whimpered, I was so wound up.

"Any chance of somebody seeing us heading to my place?" I asked him low enough that only he could hear.

"I can say I helped you unload something from the bar."

I snorted. "On our bikes?"

He groaned. "Fuck, I don't know. We'll deal with it if it even comes up."

I thought about how Mal asked me to look out for Smoke and was easily able to come up with a decent excuse for why he'd follow me home. And now I was twisting that request around. It almost felt like a betrayal. I shoved it out of my brain.

"Sounds about right," I said. "Now, let's get through this shift."

The rest of the night I sported a semi-hard-on.

CHAPTER EIGHT
SMOKE

The end of the night couldn't come soon enough. We were both adults, knew how to handle a one-night stand. Big fucking deal. We'd get each other off and hopefully douse the fire that seemed to be consuming us.

Still, I'd admit to having reservations all night long and had even considered backing out. But all I had to do was look at him—his wine-stained lips and beefed up forearms. Plus, just seeing that devious grin on his face when he was flirting with those customers made me want to push him against the bar and claim him with my mouth.

As the clocked ticked past midnight, I was nearly blind with lust for the man.

After Cherry and Lewis left, we finished emptying the trash bins, barely uttering a word, the air between us so thick I was choking on the fumes.

Finally, Vaughn cut the lights.

"I'll meet you there," he said. "I'm cool if you decide not to—"

"See you in a few," I said without hesitation. I stared at his ass moving in those jeans as he headed out the door.

When I got to his place, my stomach solidified into a tight fist. I chewed my lip all the way up the stairs and looked down at my feet once he closed the door behind me.

Vaughn's fingers hooked around the back of my neck, tugging my forehead against his. "You having second thoughts?"

"Nah, just nerves."

"Afraid of not turning me on?" he asked, panting. "Because fuck, Smoke, I'm ready to rub one out every time you look at me."

A moan burst from my throat, and my mouth brushed back and forth against his. My tongue flicked out to swipe his lips, top then bottom, as he hummed his approval.

He backed me up. My shoulder hit the door as my tongue slid past his lips, delving into his mouth. His fingers tightened around my nape as his other hand roamed my chest, tweaking a hardened nipple through my shirt.

"Fuck, I'm going to come just from kissing you," I said.

"Same here," Vaughn said, releasing a breath and then dragging his mouth away. "Maybe I need to invite you inside and offer you a drink or something."

"I'd take you up on that offer." I took a deep breath and pushed away from the door. I looked around the apartment and saw that it was nicely laid out with black leather couches, modern paintings, and a large cream area rug. "Nice place."

"Thanks."

I heard a mewling sound, and then a small black cat jumped off the chair and stretched her hind legs.

"That's Betty," Vaughn said.

My eyes darted to his. "I didn't take you to be an animal lover."

He smirked. "No? Well, I have two cats, a male and a female. The other one is gray. His name is Hurricane. Cane for short."

I guess you found out a lot about a man when you visited his private home. Last year he'd taken in Cory and Jude's dog named Chopper, and now I understood why he'd made the offer.

I followed Vaughn into his kitchen, where he pulled open the refrigerator door and grabbed two sodas. As he straightened, I slid my body against his and whispered in his ear. "You've got one of the nicest asses I've ever seen."

"Likewise," he said, shuddering. "I'd say I'd like to fuck yours, but I guess I'll have to settle for just sucking you off."

"I wouldn't complain," I said, grabbing the soda and popping the lid. I took a large gulp as Vaughn moved to the couch and sat down with his drink.

"This is a great fireplace," I said, running my hand along the mantel. "Wood-burning?"

"Gas," he said. "Think you could make me something to hang in that space above?"

"That could be arranged," I said, noticing his modern decor throughout the apartment. "Think about what you want and let me know. I'm figuring something contemporary."

"Sounds about right. The exact opposite of my pop's place with all of those antiques," he said. "He's got a thing for timepieces."

"Is that right?" My eyes darted to the art deco clock hanging on his wall. I noted that it was after two in the morning. I was used to these hours, and I knew he was, too. Still, he probably needed his rest.

"You're free to walk out of here any time, Smoke," he said as if noticing that I was thinking too damn hard.

"I know I am," I said, sitting down next to him, and wondering again what the fuck my problem was. As soon as our thighs brushed, my blood pumped straight to my groin.

"If I'd met you at a bar," he said, "we'd already be in my bed with come on the sheets."

"Same here," I said. "Though I haven't met anybody at a bar in a long time."

"Yeah?" he said, and I knew he wanted to ask more, but he held himself in check.

"So, what's holding you back now?" he asked, his fingers rubbing circles on my thigh.

I watched his large palm work wonders on my libido. "This is different."

His knuckles trailed up my arm. "Different how?"

"I know you," I said. "Have to see you practically every day."

"Yeah, but after tonight," he said, leaning forward, his finger snaking to the shell of my ear, "we can go about our business."

"That's where I start to get jumpy," I said, practically moaning from the contact. His hands were warm and rough. This was so different from being with a woman. "I want us to be friendly. Know more about each other if we have to work together. Don't want to fuck anything up."

"I feel the same." Vaughn grazed his lips right below my ear, making me shiver. "How about we agree that we won't let it be awkward?"

He stared into my eyes, and just as I nodded my approval, Vaughn sank to his knees in front of me.

"You don't have to reciprocate," he said. "I only want the opportunity to touch you. Put my mouth on you." Before I could think, he had my pants unbuttoned and the zipper down. "That'll fuel my fantasies for weeks to come."

When he palmed my cock through the material, I groaned.

He swung his face closer to my groin. "Do you want me to taste you?"

My hand reached out to touch his jaw. I liked feeling the roughness there. "Hell yes."

He dragged my pants down to my knees along with my underwear, and my dick sprang free. "Damn, I knew your cock would be something to see."

"Yeah?" I said, panting openly from the contact. "I've been dreaming about yours ever since I saw it that one morning."

His gaze was filled with pure lust, and it nearly stole my breath.

"I want to see it again," I said.

He stood up immediately and toed off his shoes. I stopped his hands from reaching for his waistband.

"Let me." I unsnapped his jeans and yanked them down. There it was, as thick and hard as I remembered it. "Damn."

Before I could take a closer look, he was back on his knees in front of me. I couldn't resist grabbing his neck and hauling him toward me. I needed to feel his lips on mine again. I yanked at his hair and he lifted up to sink against me on the couch, rubbing our cocks together. It felt so damn good, I could've come from that contact alone.

Vaughn's groin slid with perfect friction against mine as my hips began thrusting upward to match his rhythm. He groaned deep in his throat, and I loved hearing that sound coming from him.

"Fuck, I love that mouth of yours," he said, wrenching his lips away and sitting back on his heels again. "But I need to taste you."

He didn't waste any time as he bent his head and licked a circle around my crown. His fist latched solidly onto my length. I hissed as he dragged his tongue along the underside of my head, where I was most sensitive.

"Holy shit." I sagged against the cushion as my thighs shook, barely able to hang on now that his wet tongue was doing amazing things to my cock. "I'm not sure how much more I can take. Been wanting this for too damn long."

His lips engulfed my hardness. His tongue ran the length of my vein, down to where his palm smoothed over my balls. It was the perfect mix of hot mouth, soft tongue, and steady hand, and I was in fucking ecstasy.

When he sank lower, tongued my sac, and then blew a gust of air across my balls, I nearly sprang off the couch. The contrast of hot lips and cool breath had me babbling unintelligibly. His firm grip was pumping and my balls were in his mouth and I was already slipping off the edge.

My hands fisted tightly in his hair, and his eyes sprang up to mine. He kept his gaze on me while he moved his lips back to my head and licked the underside of my crown again. My spine tingled and my balls pulled up tight.

"I want you to say my name when you come," he growled.

His warm mouth surrounded me as his finger reached beneath my balls to my taint. He rubbed my sensitive skin and hummed, the vibration from his throat sending me skyrocketing to the moon.

"Fuck, Vaughn," I called out as I shot my load down his throat. He swallowed every damn drop, some of it slipping out of the side of his mouth, and he licked at the white droplets as if savoring them.

I sank against the cushions, my legs quivering and my chest heaving. He leaned over and kissed my lips. The tips of our tongues met, and I could taste myself on him.

"Having a bit of trouble moving right now," I said, and he laughed. "That was amazing."

"I agree." He pushed to his feet, sliding out of his pants. "Your cock is incredible."

He tugged his shirt over his neck, and his cock jutted upward toward his stomach. The head was practically purple and leaking against his abdomen.

"I'm going to jump in the shower. You're free to stay right there. Or if you need to take off, I won't be offended."

He strode down the hallway, his tight ass on full display, and my shaft was already filling back up. Damn, he was sexy. And he wasn't expecting anything from me. He'd said he only wanted to taste me. Well, fuck, what if I needed to taste him, too?

Catching my breath, I stood on wobbly legs. That was the hardest I'd come in a long time. I stepped out of my jeans and kicked them to the side. Then I ripped off my shirt. I followed the sound of the water down the hall.

I entered the bathroom, which was decorated in darker blue tones with tan accents. I didn't get far in my perusal because Vaughn's naked form was directly in my view, his head beneath the showerhead, his forehead leaning against the tile in front of him.

It looked like either he was trying to hold it together or he was decompressing after what he'd done. I hoped he didn't have any regrets, and I considered backing away until I saw his hands shaking and his full erection practically leaking all over the floor.

That's when I knew he was suffering in silence, so I padded inside, careful not to startle him. He briefly looked over his shoulder, the lust in his gaze blistering. I stepped flush against him, my front to his back. Without hesitation, I wrapped my hand around his hardness. He exhaled an erratic breath and released a muffled plea.

I kissed his ear. "Let me take care of you."

"Thank fuck." His hand reached out to grip the wall while I stroked him up and down.

I continued sucking on his neck while he thrust into my hand.

I flipped him around, his shoulders hitting the tiles, and seized his mouth in a searing kiss, sucking his lower lip into my mouth. His hands groped my chest and then rounded my waist to squeeze my ass.

I opened my eyes to marvel at his expression. His eyes were screwed shut and he was panting openly against my jaw.

"I love your mouth. Even this small mark right here." I swiped my tongue across his scar as he gasped and then bit my lip on a growl. His snapped his hips forward, rubbing his hard cock against mine.

I sank to my knees in front of him. "Fuck yeah," he grunted out.

He was so far gone that all it took was my tongue in his slit and my mouth consuming his shaft. "Ah, hell," he groaned as his thighs quivered.

My forearm pinned his hip so he wouldn't crumple in a heap while his come spurted down my throat. Damn, I loved everything about being with Vaughn, even the bittersweet taste of his seed. That glazed look in his eyes from what I'd just done to him had taken this experience to a whole new level.

CHAPTER NINE
VAUGHN

I woke up in the late morning neither satiated nor satisfied, my cock lying hard against my thigh. I wished I'd had the balls to ask Smoke to spend the night. Then maybe he could've fucked me so hard into my bed that it left me reeling and sated.

Instead I wanted his mouth on me again, his hard body against mine, like it'd been in the shower. And fuck, the way those heart-shaped lips wrapped around me and then took me all the way back to his throat? Damn. I'd already been skating sharply along the edge after smelling his skin and hearing his raw voice as he moaned my name.

I'd been so blissed out on Smoke, I would've taken my own cock in hand after another minute in the shower had he not joined me. But I also wanted to give him the option to leave, especially if he still had his doubts. I'd meant what I said. I simply wanted a taste of him.

I rolled over in bed and wished that his scent were buried in the very fibers of my sheets. But that would've also sucked. To smell him and not be able to have him again. It had almost been like an unspoken agreement that we didn't take it further than we had last night. We were merely testing the waters. To see what would be enough to satisfy.

I didn't know what was going through his head, but last night hadn't been enough for me, and that was my biggest fear. He was worried it would become awkward. I was troubled that I'd only want more.

Smoke wasn't due at the bar tonight, and he let slip that he'd be over at the Scorpions clubhouse. Like Mal, I wondered if this favor was asking too much of him, especially if it stirred up ugly shit from his past.

The reprieve from working in proximity to him would be a good thing, though. Might help get my brain screwed back on straight.

We couldn't be anything more to each other, anyway, even regular fuck buddies, because of our status with the club. The blowback might've been less for me because I wasn't sworn to any brotherhood. But I ran the Disciples bar, and if anybody caught wind, I didn't know what that would mean for business.

On my way to the Hog's Den, I stopped by my pop's house, comforted by the sound of the ticking timepieces when I stepped inside. The noise seemed to ground me, helped me reflect on the important things right in front of me. Pop was still his cranky self, but at least he was out of his chair and polishing an antique vase from one of the shelves.

"What brought this on?" I asked, startling him.

"Today was our anniversary," he said, swiping at the shiny brass.

"Your wedding anniversary?" I asked, wondering if he was losing it. I knew the annual reminder had already come and gone a couple months back.

"The anniversary of our first date," he said, and as he swallowed the lump in his throat, I sat down. "I took her to a movie and then a burger joint. She was wearing a blue shirt that matched her eyes."

My heart descended to my ribcage. "I know you miss her, Pop."

"Every single day," he said, rubbing the metal harder.

"Was that one of her favorites?" I asked, reaching out and pressing my hand along the smooth side.

"I bought it for her our first year of marriage," he said, still not meeting my eyes.

We sat in silence for a few minutes as I considered their relationship. Leanne had treated me as her own and put up with all my garbage in high school as I tried to figure out who the hell I was. My first male crush had been on my friend Z. She knew I was struggling through something, and would quietly rub my back while my head was buried beneath my pillow.

She and my pop were connected in ways I only marveled at, even through their ridiculous arguments about finances, when Pop wanted to add one more thing to his collection. They were rarely away from one another, and he stayed by her side in hospice until the very end.

"Why don't we take a ride out to the cemetery, Pop?"

He looked up suddenly to meet my eyes. "Now?"

"Sure, why not?" I said, standing up and motioning for him to follow. "We can stop on the way to pick up your meds and get some flowers for her gravestone."

* * *

After the afternoon with my pop, I headed in to work.

Jonas came barreling through the door as I took inventory of the juices we used for mixed drinks. "You seen Smoke around?"

"Not since last night."

That lone sentence made my chest fire up. Jonas would have no clue I meant that in more ways than one.

"Everything okay?" I asked, because he looked kind of worried, which in turn made me way anxious. I might've had only a one-night stand with Smoke, but I wasn't exactly ready to check him out of my life.

"Yeah, cool," he said as if trying to tone down his unease. "He's just running late for our meeting."

Hmmm, that didn't seem like him at all. Smoke was quiet, a hard worker, and definitely dependable.

In another hour, the Hog's Den became packed, and I could've used help behind the bar. Maybe I'd ask Mal to add one more night to Smoke's workweek.

I had to force myself not to look at that back room every five minutes, wondering if Jonas had found Smoke yet.

Later in the evening, Jude stopped in from The Board Room, the shop he worked at next door, to order takeout for Cory and him. Or, as he called it in his British vernacular, *takeaway*.

"You good?" I asked.

"Brilliant."

There used to be a time when you'd be hard pressed to get any information out of Jude, so to have him respond so positively was pretty cool. I was happy for him, because his life had been shit. I felt that familiar tug of jealousy that he could be out in the open with Cory, but that was ridiculous.

I knew what this was with Smoke. Plain and simple.

"No Smoke tonight?" he asked.

I schooled my features. "Nope."

"That's a shame," he said out of the customers' earshot. "I like seeing him back there with you."

"Don't go getting any crazy ideas," I said.

He cracked a smile and waved as he headed out the door.

Just as I was closing for the night, Smoke came blazing through the back room and headed behind the bar, straight for the tequila.

I could tell right away that something was off. His eyes almost looked haunted, and his fingers were trembling as he reached for the bottle.

"Mind if I take a shot?" he asked.

"Sure thing," I said, leaning against the bar, watching him closely.

This would count as the one and only time I'd witnessed Smoke take a drink. Something must've gone wrong tonight.

It was none of my business, and I was pretty certain he wouldn't want me on his case, so I kept my trap shut.

He downed the drink in one gulp and I held a lime slice out to him, which he grabbed gratefully before sucking on it and wincing. I tried not to stare at his mouth and imagine those full lips around my cock again.

"You want another?" I asked, holding up the bottle.

"No, I'm good." He sagged against the counter, his fingers rushing through his hair. "Tastes as shitty as I remember."

I laughed. "Booze is usually an acquired taste."

He didn't respond, he was so lost in his own head. So I figured I'd leave him alone. I cut the lights and headed toward the door.

"Stay as long as you like," I said. When I turned to look at him, something jumped in his gaze. "For whatever it's worth? You need something to take the edge off, come find me anytime, yeah?"

Without even waiting for a response, I went out the front entrance and climbed on my bike. I had a desperate need to hold him, comfort him, be whatever the hell he needed right then. That wasn't what this was between us. Still, I considered him a friend. I hightailed it out of there before I got any more ridiculous notions.

At home, I filled the cat's water bowl and hopped in the shower. It felt good to wash off the grime of a busy night.

Just as I was drying off, there was a knock on my door. My heart leapt to my throat.

I threw on a pair of sweats and headed to my entryway. I spotted Smoke through the peephole, his hands shoved stiffly in his pockets. He looked vulnerable and hesitant, and that made me swing open the door in a rush.

He practically stumbled inside and fell right into my arms. I pulled his body flush against mine and rubbed the back of his head. It felt so intimate that my stomach tightened at the tenderness of the moment.

I loved the idea that he had sought me out, of all people. But this was about something else altogether. I knew that. And if I could provide that for him, so be it.

My lips found his ear. "Whatever you need, name it."

He eyes sprang to mine, and a spark ignited in them. His cinnamon breath fanned across my lips. "I...I need to get lost. Forget for a while."

I considered asking him exactly what he needed to forget, but I didn't want to ruin the moment. He needed me right now. Needed my hands on him. He hadn't pursued anybody else, man or woman. Another warm body.

"You got it," I said, and then my hand clamped around his neck as I dragged his lips to mine, kissing him long and deep. He moaned into my mouth and swayed against me.

My fingers fumbled for the zipper on his jeans, and I yanked it down. I sank to my knees and pushed him back against the door for leverage. His cock was so enticing as it curved upward and leaked from the tip that my mouth was on him in an instant. I licked the head and sucked lightly on the crown as my own cock responded in my pants.

"Wait," he said in a hoarse voice. "I want to feel you naked next to me."

I stood up. "No need to ask twice."

I pushed my sweats down my hips as his eyes widened and then glazed over. I'd forgotten that I'd just come from the shower and had gone commando. He licked his lips as he stared down at my cock, which was hardening by the second.

He got busy removing the rest of his clothes, leaving a trail as he followed me down the hall to my bedroom.

At my door, he slid behind me and palmed my cheeks, groaning into my neck. "Damn that ass of yours."

Simply hearing that raspy voice made me shudder. As soon as I turned, his mouth was on me, gripping my neck. He pushed his groin against mine. Our tongues battled to sample and lick and taste and after several long minutes, I dragged my mouth away to catch my breath, resting my forehead against his.

I reached down to swipe my thumb against the bead of pre-come on his cock and then sucked on it. "Mmmm…you taste good."

He growled, yanked my face to his, and sank his tongue deeply inside my mouth.

We fell back on the bed, him on top, grinding his cock alongside mine.

He had sought me out tonight, so I wasn't going to beg him to fuck me. I wasn't even sure if that was what he wanted. He might have shown up here, but maybe we were still pretending that if we did everything but the dirty deed, it wouldn't count as much.

I seized his thighs and hauled him toward my chest. After another second, he got the idea, straddling me so that his cock was sitting directly against my mouth.

"Fuck," he said as I licked up and down the underside of his vein before grasping him in my fist and swallowing him whole. The noises coming from his throat made me squirm and moan as he pumped his hips and expertly fucked my mouth. "Goddamn, that feels incredible."

I was so turned on, smelling his spicy, manly scent as his balls slapped beneath my chin, that I was on the verge of exploding without any assistance. If he simply touched me, I'd shoot off good.

Just when I knew he was going to come, his head thrown back, his chest and neck flushed, I grabbed hold of my own straining and leaking length and yanked on it for a few long pumps.

As his come filled my mouth and slid down my throat, I felt my cock blast apart in my hand. I braced my fingers against his lower back where shots of my warm seed had landed. He groaned when he felt it hit, and I continued sucking on his length, attempting to taste every last drop.

He swiped his finger against his nape, where some of my come had apparently spurted and then plunged it deep in his mouth, tasting me. That helped rouse one final surge from my cock as my arms slid downward, completely spent.

"Fuck, that was hot," he said. He sank down on my bed, and I lay there panting beside him, unable to form any syllables in response. His hand grazed against mine on the sheets, and when I interlaced our fingers, he squeezed tight, molding out palms together.

A warmth filled my chest from the simple act of having him hold my hand. Eventually I rolled off the bed, headed to the bathroom, and returned with a wet washcloth.

"Turn over," I said, pushing at his shoulder. I wiped him down, admiring the black gothic block letters on his back that spelled out "Mitsy's." I wondered if that had been his mother's name. My fingers trailed over the inscription and then down to his firm backside. What I wouldn't give to get inside him, if only once.

Given his earlier reaction, I knew the topic would be off-limits, so why even torture myself with the thought?

When I lay back down, he tugged me into a tender kiss, his fingers at my face, his tongue exploring my mouth at a leisurely pace.

"Did that do the trick?" I asked against his perfectly shaped lips, still tasting the remnants of his cinnamon gum.

"Hell yes…thanks."

"Were you with Fish tonight?" I knew that he was supposed to be helping dig up information on his old club. Given the shadows beneath his eyes earlier, I understood why Mal had asked me to look after him.

"Yeah," he said, his fingers sliding up and down my arm as he refused eye contact with me.

"Didn't go so well?" I murmured against his ear, kissing and nuzzling his neck.

His jaw locked and his body tensed. Nothing was worth him getting so worked up. He had sought me out for release, not to relive memories.

"Never mind," I said, rubbing my fingers along his chin. "Just come here."

He easily scooted over so that I could pull him against me.

I brushed my fingers through his hair and kissed his temple, and he sighed appreciatively.

He was so beautiful, but not like an Adonis. More in a boyishly handsome kind of way. I wasn't sure I was able to say that about many guys, but I had always thought that about him. From the first moment I laid eyes on him.

I continued stroking and soothing him until he fell asleep in my arms. I watched him for long moments, staring at his slightly crooked nose, his curved lips, and his long and nearly translucent eyelashes that fanned across his cheeks.

It felt fucking incredible to have been the one to comfort him. To have him in my bed. To be the person he came to after a horrible night.

All those times over the past year I'd burned for him across the bar, I'd longed for this. To feel the weight of his body in my arms, his soft breaths against my skin.

I knew it was probably wrong to allow this to happen, to want him here. At the moment I couldn't even find it in me to give a fuck. None of that other shit mattered. For this one night, I would be his refuge, his safe harbor.

Fighting drowsiness, I closed my eyes, marveling at how good everything felt in that moment, how right. Even if we never had sex.

When I woke up the following morning, Smoke was gone.

CHAPTER TEN
SMOKE

I was in the garage at my makeshift tool bench, applying the finishing touches on a metal art sculpture for one of the brothers. He'd just moved in with his old lady and told me he needed something for his man cave. I snorted to myself. *Man cave*. What in the hell kind of term was that? I got it, though—I liked man caves as well. Christ, I was pathetic.

Using polyurethane to seal the edges, I thought about last night. Gathering intel on my former club brothers with Fish had affected me more than I'd suspected. I figured I was beyond caring, but when Fish had asked me questions about certain Asylum members, a rage had churned deep in my gut. I wanted to smash my fist into something.

Instead, I went for a long ride along the lakeside, but even that wasn't enough to clear my head. So I went to the Hog's Den. The shot was an idiot move, but it did nothing for me anyway. Only reminded me that I hated the flavor of booze, always had. Didn't even give me a buzz.

The only thing that did was Vaughn. He had allowed me to use him last night. He understood what I needed. And that right there made me feel things I shouldn't have been feeling for the guy.

Still, I didn't fuck Vaughn, even though I knew I could have. He would've let me; I saw it in his eyes. Something had held me back...again. Messing around was one thing but being inside someone, especially someone like him, was a different ballgame altogether.

That was some fucked up logic right there. I wouldn't have hesitated had it been anybody else, man or woman.

I told myself it was because I had to be around Vaughn all the time. This attraction to him had gotten out of control, almost like a fever. And I had no idea when it would pass. Maybe screwing his perfect ass would finally do it.

The truth was, I'd had a secret fuck buddy named Jake when I'd been with the Asylum. He totally messed up my head, along with the drugs, and I never wanted to get so caught up in somebody like that again. So what the hell was I doing with Vaughn?

Vaughn was nothing like Jake. But what I've done with him behind closed doors meant my ass could be out on the street again. The Disciples had become more my family than any I'd ever known, and I didn't want to do anything to blow that.

Though I knew I could make it on my own this time. I was young and lost when I had first been taken under the Asylum's wing. Mitsy's bar had just burned down, and my dad had died in that fire.

The screen door slapped open and I heard Felix's footsteps as I twisted one of the final screws in place. He always wore those brown steel-toed boots with the heavy soles, and I could hear him coming a mile away.

"Looking good, man," Felix said, heading toward his bike, his mop of light brown hair falling into his eyes.

He was my closest brother, probably because we had become recruits at the same time. He was a pretty quiet guy, even more so than me, so I was comfortable around him, even in the silence. Felix had come from a fucked up life as well, had almost been like a nomad on the road once his parents disowned him, and he apparently found his calling with the club. His loved repairing old cars and threw some good bones my way from the auto parts shop for my sculptures.

"I'm headed to the compound," he said, tossing his leg over the seat on his hog. "See you in a few?"

"Yep, right behind you." I made sure to get the final screws as tight as humanly possible so there would be no problems hanging it on the wall.

I propped the metal piece against the cement and stood back to appraise my work. I'd stopped using my hands when I was with the Asylum. I was too strung out half the time, anyway, and had completely lost myself. It wasn't until I had put in time at the auto parts store, and picked up my first piece of scrap metal from a rotor, that it all came back.

I asked the guys if I could take some of the pieces from the leftover scraps, no doubt from stolen property, so what did they care?

The guys thought I was nuts until they saw what I could create. Then they began placing orders. Mal was so impressed, he asked me to make some pieces for the bar he'd invested in, which is when I'd first laid eyes on Vaughn.

It'd been an actual physical reaction, like a gong sounding off inside my chest. And when his whiskey-brown eyes snagged mine, my dick swelled instantly. When his gaze traveled down to my bulge, I knew for certain he wasn't exactly straight.

In the following months, he'd always flirted with the ladies, so I figured he swung both ways, same as me.

I screwed the cap back on the polyurethane, cleaned up my tools, and hopped on my bike. I needed to hightail my butt over there before Mal thought I was intentionally late. He did not like tardiness. He hated it so much, I once witnessed him throwing a hubcap supplier out on his ass. Told him if he showed up late for a delivery again, Mal would take his business elsewhere.

When I rolled into the compound, which was on a sprawling property on the rural outskirts of town, I noticed most of the guys were already there. I parked in my usual spot next to Felix and headed inside.

"We all here?" Mal asked when he spotted me. "Let's get started."

A large rectangular table in the very back room was where we usually met to conduct club business. Mal and Jonas were always on opposite ends, probably so they could look to each other for confirmation on decisions. We each sat in the same spots even though seats weren't officially assigned. I was always positioned between Felix and Slim. Slim was tall as fuck and had these long, skinny legs that ate up most of the room beneath the table.

"Got your piece ready to go in my garage," I muttered to him as I sat down.

He gave me the thumbs-up. "I'll pick it up this weekend."

When everyone was seated, the room grew silent, waiting on Mal to speak. It was his ritual to look each one of us in the eye, beginning with Jonas and then moving in a clockwise direction. It was as if he was acknowledging our existence, our place in the club.

This club was run with more ceremony and order than my last one. The Asylum was pretty chaotic most of the time. There was constant booze and drugs and entertainment. It felt like being in a nightclub during all hours of the day.

Sure, there were meetings, but there were also secrets and deception. I never truly knew whom I could trust. The Disciples had tradition, shared ideals, and loyalty. Which made me feel even worse about what I was doing on the side with Vaughn.

But that was about straight-up sex, and I was going to bet that it didn't even come close to some of the crap these guys were involved in outside club business and behind closed doors. We might've ribbed each other about hookups, but we really didn't share what went on in our private lives. Especially if the guys had old ladies.

"Brothers," Mal began and lightly pounded his fist on the wooden table. "I realize it's been a hard few months trying to extricate ourselves from old messes."

We all nodded. Mal had asked some other clubs to buy him out fair and square, or trade weapons for parts, so we could come clean. A couple of old timers who'd been tight with Mal's dad had left the club early on because they thought the prez had gotten too soft. But those of us who remained were in agreement that being on the right side of the law didn't leave you spineless. We all wanted to focus on making our businesses lucrative. It meant a better and safer payoff in the end.

Sure, we still looked over our shoulders and watched our backs, but my conscience was pretty clear. Most of us even stopped regularly carrying our pieces. My blade remained in my back pocket, but that was a given.

"Those of us seated at this table are on the same page, yeah?" he asked, studying each of our expressions, just to be certain. "I couldn't be more grateful."

"Your grandfather would be proud." Jonas slapped the recruit closest to him on the back, and a few *hear hear's* were chanted around the table. Mal's grandfather had founded the Disciples decades ago. It was his father who had nearly brought it down. Mal had been raised with the influence of both but identified most with his grandfather's vision. Mal didn't share much personal business, but he had told each recruit about the origin and vision of the club.

Mal lifted his chin in thanks to Jonas. "None of us here wants any more bloodshed unless absolutely necessary. We want to make an honest living and support our families."

Some mumbled their agreement. Plenty of the guys had old ladies and kids to support, but there were also several of us who were flying solo. Still, I could only agree with him, having come from a club immersed deeply in drug possession and gun running and the danger that came with that. Fuck, I couldn't even count the number of times I almost paid with my own life for my own stupidity in joining that organization.

"Thing is, I want us to get back to our roots. Be a true club, not a gang of thugs," Mal said, clearing his throat, all side discussions ending. "Our cash reserve has taken a serious hit. Pulling out of those final arms deals will make us safer, but other organizations won't like it."

"Ran into one of the Cyclones at the deli the other day," Slim said. "Talking smack about us. Saying we were going to have to borrow some dough from other clubs to cover our overhead."

"Yeah?" Mal's jaw ticked. He leaned back in his chair. "How'd you respond?"

"Ignored him at first, but he wouldn't drop it," Slim said, shaking his head. "So I told him we'd see him when his Harley needed some fine-tuning. He'd see how lucrative the parts business was when we handed him the bill."

The guys cracked up, and a couple of the brothers fist bumped.

"Or how about when he wants a good beer and the best wings in town," Felix said. "Sorry, man, no stools available at the bar for you."

Mal smiled and placed his hands behind his head. "Bunch of dumbasses. We'll have to prove them wrong. Which means we work hard and don't cause any trouble."

He eyes flitted quickly across a new recruit named Simon who had gotten into a couple of skirmishes with another club.

"We've got leftover debts to pay," Mal said. "Not sure how to handle our deal with the chop shops, but one mess at a time. Like the operation Smoke's involved in, for instance."

Everyone's eyes sprang my way, and I nodded at Mal.

"He's a good brother, helping us out," Mal said, and his eyes held a hint of appreciation along with some discomfort. "I know you didn't want to delve back into your past, Smoke, but I will be forever grateful, my man, that you helped us repay our debt to the Scorpions."

"Hear hear," Jonas rumbled, and the guys beat their fists in succession down the line in what sounded like a rousing rhythmic rendition of a tribal chant. Guess it was our very own tune.

I smiled and tipped my chin.

Mal held up his hand. "Plus the feds are going to be interested in how the Asylum is using those gun runners to cross over the border. Might just take down their entire operation."

A sharp pinch of apprehension stabbed at my gut, and Mal could see it plainly on my face.

"No worries," Mal said for my benefit, even though he was looking over at Jonas now. "The boom won't come down on us."

So I pushed my anxiety aside. This club had my back.

"Other Disciples business?"

Felix started talking about a new shipment of bumpers at the auto store, and I felt like I was part of something that I could truly be proud of. Even if I had to hide a part of who I was. Every family had their secrets.

Chapter Eleven
Vaughn

I was at one end of the bar and Smoke was down at the other, where a group of rowdy biker chicks had set up camp on some barstools.

I could tell we were both trying like hell not to stare too long at one another or even make direct contact with our limbs. If he was anything like me, he was wound so tight from sexual tension, he was about to snap.

Why had we thought that whatever was going on between us would be resolved after a couple of encounters? Was it because he hadn't fucked my brains out yet? Or would doing so only make this—whatever this was—even worse?

Because damn it, I couldn't get the thought out of my head of Smoke staying at my place again. The heat of his skin as he lay beside me. The rough stubble on his jaw when our mouths met.

Right then, Smoke passed behind me to get to the bar glasses I'd just stacked, and his thigh skimmed past my hip. "Fuck," I murmured low.

"Tell me about it," he said as he straightened and went on his way to serve his customer.

As soon as Mal and some other Disciples showed up and occupied a table in the middle of the room, it was business as usual. We didn't even give each other a second glance.

Toward the end of the night, after the crowd had already thinned, my cell rang. I ignored it as I continued bussing a table. When it sounded off again almost immediately after, I dug it out of my pocket, nervous it was something concerning my pop.

"This is Vaughn."

My landlord so rarely called that I didn't even recognize his voice, let alone his number.

"Fuck," I said into the phone, the cold call punching a hole in my chest. "I'll be right there."

Mal's eyebrows were drawn together in concern. "Something wrong?"

"Landlord," I said, lifting my face to the ceiling, hoping to find some fresh air to lessen the anxiety swirling in my chest. "My place was broken into. I've gotta take off."

"We're cool here," Smoke said immediately, his eyes wide and round. "I'll clean and lock up."

"Thanks man," I said. As I gathered my keys and coat, Smoke moved to the middle of room to have a conversation with Mal.

I thought I lived in a pretty safe part of town, but that meant nothing when somebody was desperate.

"You need anything from us?" Mal asked.

"Nah, think I'm good," I said, lifting my arm in a wave. "Cops are on their way."

"Head over there when you're finished here," I heard Mal say to Smoke as I flew through the door.

"Will do, Prez," he said, but I couldn't even take the time to think that through.

As I swung my leg over my bike, all of my muscles had grown taut. I didn't need this shit in my life. I already wanted to maim the motherfucker. I only hoped I hadn't lost everything. Not that I had that much. But still, what I did have was earned with blood, sweat, and tears.

When I got to my place a short time later, my landlord was on the lawn with two officers. He explained how the tenant across the hall from me noticed that my door was cracked open. When she peeked inside and saw the mess, she immediately called for help.

I headed up to my place with the cops on my heels and my stomach in my throat.

The door had been left ajar just as my landlord had said, and from the doorway, I could see that my cushions had been hauled off the couch and the chairs had been toppled over.

Moving further inside, I could feel the blood draining from my face. Most of the drawers had been pulled open and my personal belongings scattered across the floor.

One of the officers stepped behind me. "Anything stolen?"

As I moved through the apartment, I saw nothing expensive missing or out of place. My television and laptop all remained surprisingly untouched. "Doesn't look that way."

I felt relieved yet confused. Had the thief been interrupted during the robbery?

In my bedroom, the nightstand drawer was pulled wide open, and condoms and lube were strewn around the place, some lying across the bed.

A distinct foul stench of piss arose from the corner of the room. What the fuck?

Somebody had broken into my place, not to rob me, but to screw with my things?

Was somebody trying to out me? Not that condoms and lube meant anything. And it wasn't like I had a stash of gay porn sitting around or something.

I looked over at the other officer, who had followed me inside the room and was staring intently at the condoms. "You got a vindictive ex on your hands?" he asked.

I rushed my fingers through my hair. "Not that I'm aware of. Shit, this is fucked up."

I mean, I'd dated over the years and had both men and women in my bed, but nobody who would want to screw with me like this.

He nodded. "I've seen plenty of weird shit over the years. Guess this would qualify. Don't get me wrong, thieves do some crazy crap when they rob a place, but it doesn't look like anything was stolen."

"So how would you classify this?" I asked, gritting my jaw.

"Someone just getting off on messing with you."

I stared at the bottle of lube lying on my pillow. "So, you think it's somebody I know?"

He was writing in his small notebook. "If not, then somebody's having some sick fun at your expense."

I squeezed the bridge of my nose. "That's fucking great."

After the police department took pictures, checked for prints, and left, I spoke to my landlord again to ask more questions. But he never saw anybody enter the building.

Plus, my door had been jarred open with some kind of tool, according to the cop. The perp obviously knew what he was doing.

I spotted my neighbor in the hall when I made my way back to my apartment. She looked concerned, probably for her own safety as well. I told her, "If it's any consolation, the officer said it might be somebody I know."

"I'm sorry," she said before she shut her door and slid the latch firmly in place.

When I re-entered my apartment, I heard a soft mewling sound. Fuck, my cats. If only they could talk, they'd tell me who did this. And then I'd string the guy up by the balls.

The first to peek his head from beneath the couch was Cane. "Come here, buddy."

He was trembling. I picked him up and curled him in my arms to soothe him. Or was it the other way around? This whole thing had completely unnerved me. After I found my other cat's hiding place in the hall closet and made sure they were both okay, I began picking up the overturned chairs in my living room, fuming the entire time.

I'd heard about people feeling violated when they'd been robbed, but this was the first time I'd understood the feeling. Hell, somebody had been in my apartment and put their grimy hands all over my things. And then they took a piss in the corner of my bedroom. What kind of sick fuck did something like that?

When my buzzer rang, it was pretty late, and by that time I was already placing sheets on my couch so I could sleep near the door with one eye open.

"Who is it?" I asked wearily into the intercom.

"Smoke."

Relief washed through me, but I wasn't sure why. Maybe because he had come all the way over here to check on me, even though I knew he had been given the task by Mal. Would he have shown up on his own anyway? I'd like to think that we'd come to an understanding, that maybe we considered each other friends.

"C'mon up," I said and then pushed the button to release the door. I couldn't help wondering if that was exactly how this guy had gotten into my place, behind a stranger entering the building. I almost felt like a chicken-shit for being so shaken up since I knew if anybody tried breaking into my joint while I was home, I could take him down with one vicious punch. So maybe it was the exhaustion and rage that was making me sappy.

When Smoke stepped inside, he quickly scanned the room. It had mostly been tidied up, so it probably didn't look to him like anything had gone down. I hadn't touched the bedroom yet. I didn't want to fucking step foot in there. Not tonight.

"So what the hell happened?" he asked after I shut the door behind him.

"Someone got inside and ransacked my place," I said. "I just got done cleaning most of it up."

"Anything stolen?" He looked pointedly at the television.

"Nope," I said and then walked over to the couch to finish adjusting the pillows.

He stepped further into the room. "Then why…"

"Knocked stuff around," I said, motioning with my hand. "And in the bedroom…"

"What?" he narrowed his eyes after I turned away from him and clenched my fists.

"Go see for yourself."

He walked past me down the hall and threw open the door.

"Well, fuck."

CHAPTER TWELVE
SMOKE

Was that piss I smelled?

The nightstand drawer had been thrown open, and condoms were strewn on the floor and across the bed.

I looked for the source of the stench and found it in the corner near the closet door. Something about the very act of it jabbed deep inside my gut.

"Shit, Vaughn," I said loud enough for him to hear. "This is really messed up."

"Tell me something I don't already know," he said from the hallway, as if keeping his distance. I didn't blame him. But this was his home, and for him to not feel comfortable here made rage swirl inside of me. "I don't even want to go in there. What else did that fucker do? Rub his bare ass on my sheets?"

No way in hell I'd tell him my suspicions and how close he might've been to the truth.

"Is that why you were setting up to sleep on your couch?" I asked, backing out of the room.

"Damn straight." I heard him shuffling some things around, getting ready for some needed shuteye. If he was even able to sleep after all of this. "I'll deal with the rest in the morning."

My phone chirped, and I fished it out of my pocket.

"Hey Mal. Just got to Vaughn's," I said, knowing he'd want an update before he nodded off as well. "Someone broke in and wrecked the joint."

"His stuff stolen?" Mal asked.

"No, not a thing," I said in a disgusted voice.

There was a long, drawn-out silence. Mal was familiar with these kind of stunts. This was more personal.

"Was it somebody he knew?"

I looked at Vaughn and saw the anger and despair brewing behind his gaze.

"I'm not entirely sure," I said.

"You think it's his affiliation with our club?" he asked. "You got a line on this one?"

"Maybe," I said, not yet willing to share my suspicions. "I'll ask around."

"You do that. Let me know what you find," he said. "Tell Vaughn he's welcome to stay at the compound for the night."

Vaughn was pacing in his kitchen like a caged animal as if ready to be on the defensive, but still listening intently to our conversation.

"It's too late to have him drive up there." I walked over to Vaughn and placed my hand on his shoulder. After he startled, he seemed to sag into my touch. "My guest room's a mess, so I'll have him sleep on my couch."

Vaughn stared at me, mouth agape, and I raised my eyebrows to tell him there'd be no discussion. Though he kept his composure, the gratitude was apparent in his eyes. I didn't want him to feel alone right now. Because I'd felt that way too many times to count. It helped to know that somebody had your back.

"Okay, keep me posted," Mal said.

"Will do," I said, squeezing Vaughn's shoulder and then dropping my hand.

"And Smoke?" Mal said. "You need to keep tabs on him until we figure this out."

As if I wasn't already overly involved in this man's life.

Mal took a deep breath. "We consider him one of our own."

"Will do. And Prez?" I said, thinking about Vaughn's bedroom, which would be rancid by morning. "Let's get the cleaning service out here to scour this place top to bottom first thing in the morning?"

"That bad?"

"You don't want to know."

I clicked the End button and turned to Vaughn. "Get your things. You're coming with me."

He arched an eyebrow. "Pretty bossy tonight, aren't you?"

I looked over his shoulder to his makeshift bed on the couch. "You're not sleeping here. Not tonight."

He stared hard at me for a long moment and finally nodded. "Thanks."

He slid on his boots and grabbed his keys. Before he left, he filled that small paw print water bowl in the kitchen. He had been the vulnerable one tonight, the guy whose place had been broken into. Yet he still made sure to take care of those cats. Just like he took care of his regulars at the bar. And took care of me, when I had come calling the other day.

We didn't talk on the way down to our bikes, each of us lost in our own heads. I looked around the neighborhood and kept my eyes peeled as we left. I couldn't help the sinking feeling that this might've had something to do with me.

When we got to my place, I directed Vaughn to pull inside the garage next to my bike. Felix's Chevelle, which he'd helped build from the ground up, was parked in the other spot, next to my workbench.

Vaughn eyed it appreciatively. "Cool ride."

"Felix's pride and joy."

He was still out on patrol, but I'd already sent him a text about Vaughn staying upstairs with me. Fuck the couch. I could see the fatigue and frustration in Vaughn's posture. I wanted him in my bed.

After I locked the door behind him, he looked around my apartment. "Nice."

"You think so?" I said, to make conversation and rid myself of the sudden case of nerves. "Thanks."

I had never been one for decorating. I just got myself decent furniture and kept my place clean. But right then, it mattered what Vaughn thought of how I lived. Why it mattered so much, I didn't know.

"Can I get you anything?" I asked as Vaughn toed off his shoes and carefully placed his keys on my coffee table, as if mindful of nicking it.

"No, I'm good," he said as he sat down on the black leather cushion. "Your couch looks comfy. I'm just gonna crash if that's okay with you."

My eyebrows lifted to my hairline. "Seriously?"

His fingers absently traced over the curve of one of the pillows. "What?"

"I know what I told Mal, but I wouldn't make you sleep on my couch."

He bit his lip. "I thought maybe you…"

His words stalled as I stalked over to him and bent down to his eye level.

"You thought wrong," I rumbled. "And you had a hard night, so I'm okay if all you want to do is sleep."

He grasped my cheek and then tightened his fingers against my hairline. "What I want to do is *forget.*"

CHAPTER THIRTEEN
SMOKE

I panted from the close contact, the heat of his hand, the turmoil in his eyes. "I can help you with that, too."

And then my mouth collided with his, our tongues flicking and winding around one another, as I attempted to rein in my unsteady pulse. I urged his shoulders back on the couch and sank down on top, my hardness grinding against his.

My hands curved his hips and then dug beneath to grasp at his ass. I squeezed the perfect roundness as he thrust his hips upward, driving me wild. It felt so damn perfect to be next to him again, to have him in my space this time. If he wanted to lose himself in me, I'd be more than glad to assist.

I lifted my chest just enough to tear his T-shirt over his head. My lips drifted over his throat and collarbone, tasting his salty skin, and then downward to swipe my tongue across his pec. His nipples were like unblemished pennies, and they swelled from my lips and teeth licking and biting them. He moaned and writhed, his mouth lifting to suck hungrily at my neck.

"Fuck," I said, groaning and squirming out of his hold even though it felt so good. "You can't leave a mark."

"I don't give a damn," Vaughn snapped but then pulled away and practically ripped my shirt over my shoulders. He threw it to the floor and then attacked my collarbone instead. "I want you to remember whose mouth was on you."

"Believe me," I practically whimpered from the roughness of his chin dragging across my skin. "I won't *ever* forget."

His widened eyes darted up to mine, and I stared back, unashamed of what I'd confessed. Because right then and there, he was the sexiest man I'd ever laid eyes on.

I sat back on my heels, catching my runaway breaths and gazing at the hard planes of his flawless torso. How his hipbones protruded above the curve of his abdominal muscles and his perfect copper nipples were glossy from my mouth.

I reached for his hands to yank him up and led him down the hall to my bedroom. Before he could get a good look around, I shoved him against the door and devoured his lips again, my tongue swiping across that jagged scar more than once. His fingers raked through my hair while I pinned my groin to his. I had never wanted to be inside somebody more than in that moment.

He fumbled to unsnap the button on my pants. I did the same with his, and we turned toward my bed. The thought of fucking the horrible night out of his head transformed into uncontrollable need.

I wrenched his zipper open and yanked his pants partway down his hips. As soon as I saw that tight ass peeking from beneath the material, I flipped him over and pushed his hips firmly to the bed. The denim was cutting into the top of his thighs, but I was already kneeling on the floor behind him and parting his cheeks, my finger trailing his crease.

"Ah, fuck," he said, struggling against me. "What the hell?"

"Sorry, couldn't wait," I said, looking at that perfect tan hole. My cock thickened in my pants. "I need to taste this ass and then ram my dick so hard inside of you, you'll be walking funny for days."

"Holy fuck. You get me so damn cranked up," he grunted. "You keep talking like that and I'll spurt all over your sheets."

"You'll come when I say you're ready," I rumbled and then licked a trail across his lower back. Vaughn shuddered and ground his feet into the carpet, seeking purchase.

"Suppose this is a side to you I haven't seen." His eyes darkened and his gaze turned feral as he glanced back at me.

"Maybe so. Guess you'll find out." I could tell he was used to being in charge, but he wouldn't be with me. Not this time. Though I'd admit it turned me way the hell on to imagine what it might be like with him in control. The other night might've been a sample when I'd come to his place so dejected.

But tonight. Tonight he needed me to tell him what to do and to take him to that blissed out place.

I dragged his jeans the rest of the way down and tossed them aside. "Now shut the hell up so I can get my tongue inside you."

His gasp was followed by a long moan as I ripped open his cheeks and shoved my tongue at his puckered furrow. I delivered long licks up and down and then circled around his channel while unintelligible words fell from his lips.

"Goddamn, such a perfect little hole," I said, niggling the edge of my thumb there. Never in my life had I wanted to get inside another man like this. I wanted to devour every single inch of him. And that's exactly what I did with my lips and tongue until he was shivering with raw desire.

He fisted the blankets with a savage grip, thrust out his ass, and growled like some ferocious animal, all because I was making him crazy. I fucking loved it.

The skin around his hole was slick and softened from my mouth, and I blew a cool breath across the crease.

"Uuuuhhh, what the hell are you doing to me?" he grunted, his thighs trembling. "Can't take much more. Need...need to feel you inside me. Need it so bad."

His hips were grinding into the sheets, and I was leaking so damn bad I needed release. With one hand I unzipped my jeans and pushed them down my hips before I nutted right inside my pants.

"My tongue first," I grunted, and he groaned, smashing his face into the pillow. I pressed the tip against his hole, nudging it inside until I could get deeper. He cried out.

"Yeah, that's it," I said, giving him a short breather. "I love tasting you from the inside."

I added a finger alongside my tongue and stretched him wider as his ass muscles clenched and quivered against my jaw.

"I can't…oh fuck, I can't…" His balls slapped my chin as he thrust backward. They were firm and engorged, and I could feel my own sac prickling and lifting.

Another minute more and my mouth released him. He sagged into the mattress and muttered at the loss of fullness there. "Gonna fuck you now," I said.

"About damn time," he growled, looking back at me. His lips were plump and plum-stained and his eyes were practically slits, so glazed over with lust.

"You telling me you didn't like that?" I slapped his ass and he practically whimpered.

"I fucking loved it," he said as I rolled a condom over my length and applied the lube generously, so close to coming from my own hand.

I sank down on top of him, feeling his damp skin and kissing his musky neck. I needed to feel his body next to mine. Dragging his jaw back for a steamy kiss, I lined up my cock to his hole.

Biting down hard on his shoulder, I nudged inside him. He moaned and swore and clenched his cheeks as he attempted to adjust to my girth.

I lost my breath as spikes of pleasure rushed straight to my groin. I couldn't move. He felt so fucking unbelievable. The room appeared to slant and waver as sweat pooled along my hairline.

"Oh fuck," Vaughn choked out. I gripped his hips, attempting to harness the bolt of lightening that shot through me as I pressed forward.

Electric heat licked over my skin, and I looked down at my cock buried halfway inside him. I didn't want to come too quickly, because hell if I knew whether I'd get this chance with him again. And I wanted to. Fuck, I wanted to.

I slung my arm around his chest and anchored him to me, groaning into his shoulder. It felt so intimate right then and he must've felt it, too, because his hand slid across the length of my arm and interlocked with mine. My chest felt strangely tight as he squeezed my fingers.

It was fucked up for sure how I was feeling about this man. Like I needed to possess all of him. Needed him to know, at least for tonight, that he was mine.

"Vaughn." My other hand slinked down to grasp at his hip, and I began pumping with long smooth strokes. "You feel that? You feel how deep I am inside you?"

"Fuck yeah, I feel you," he bit out through clenched teeth. My hand moved from his hip to tangle in Vaughn's hair. "It's goddamn amazing."

My thighs thrust forward in powerful strides as we moved in unison for several long moments. The only sound in the room was our breaths and grunts and gasps.

"You want more of this cock?" I said in his ear, biting and licking the skin beneath. "You want more of me?"

"Yeah," he said, almost in a sob. "I need more, goddammit."

My fingers rounded his thigh, and I seized hold of his cock. I slicked my thumb over the layer of pre-come that had pooled on his head and pumped him firmly. His fingers settled over mine as we pleasured him together.

"I'm so damn close," he whispered, his head falling to my shoulder, his labored breaths bursting toward the ceiling. "Please. I need you to fuck me harder."

At those words, I released him, and his forearm sank down on the bed while he continued yanking on his own length. His ass looked perfectly laid out in front of me, my cock buried deep inside.

I let out a loud growl like some damn gorilla claiming the jungle. My jungle. I was all raw nerves and sensation, and I rammed him with a ferocity I didn't even know I possessed.

I floated onto some other kind of plane. I heard Vaughn announce that he was coming, and I felt his guttural release as long spirals of semen gushed all over my sheets.

But I was somewhere in a different universe. "So good, so good, it's never been so—"

A cry wrenched from my throat as my back arched and stiffened and I unloaded inside of him. Hot seed continued propelling from me as I gasped and shook, my cock seeming to contract involuntarily.

I sagged on top and panted heavily into his neck. My arms encircled him as I slowly regained my capacity to breathe.

Chapter Fourteen
Smoke

We lay in a heap of our own sweat and come, our bodies relaxing by varying degrees. Vaughn looked thoroughly fucked, and I didn't want to admit to myself that I had never had better than him.

Finally, I got up to throw away my condom and wet a washcloth. I wiped him down as he lay on his side, nearly comatose. I gently kissed his lips as he smiled lazily, running his thumb along the scruff on my chin. I would remember that sated and sexy grin on my worst days.

I slid behind him on the sheets and then scooted forward to drape my arm over his hip. It felt so fucking good to have him in my bed.

My eyes closed, and I was just about to drift off to sleep when he prodded my arm. "What's up?" I mumbled.

"Why did you seem so freaked inside my bedroom tonight?" he asked in a groggy voice.

My shoulders stiffened. "Because of the condoms and shit that fucker had thrown around."

"Nah, man, it was more than that," he said, and I wondered whether it was worth it to lie to him. He knew something was up. He was good at reading my body language. Was always good at it. "You seriously looked spooked."

I rushed my fingers through my hair. "Fuck. Listen, it looked familiar to me."

He rolled over to study me. "What did?"

His eyes were boring into mine and I had to glance elsewhere. "The scene…the setup."

He grasped my jaw, forcing my gaze to his. "What the fuck does that mean?"

"It…I think…it might've been my ex, okay?" I shot straight up, suddenly enraged and remorseful over what I'd confessed. Even the idea of it was unbelievable. My feet landed on the cool floor, and I headed to the hallway.

"What the hell are you talking about?" he asked, following me into the kitchen, where I pulled out a water bottle and gulped practically the entire thing down. "What ex?"

I handed him some water. As he cracked it open, I sagged against the counter, which cooled my heated skin. "I had a secret relationship with one of the Asylum. Guy by the name of Jake."

His gaze snapped up to mine. "Jake the Snake?"

I cringed over the nickname, which actually fit him well. Apparently he was first given the moniker because of what he was housing down below, but later it came to mean how he dealt with club business. "So you've heard of him?"

"Yeah, man. Not much," he said, after gulping water. "But enough to know he's hardcore."

"Well, now you know why I think it might be him," I said, wiping my mouth against my forearm. "He would…leave his mark after he'd do a job. He thought it was funny. Like a dominance kind of thing."

Vaughn recoiled from me and headed back to the bedroom. I watched his tight ass all the way down my hallway as I followed him.

"Did anybody find out?" he asked after he sank back down in bed and pulled the sheet to his waist. His eyes were weary and red-rimmed. "About the two of you?"

"Hell no," I said. "At least, I don't think so. We kept it private. We were careful. The guys thought he was showing me the ropes."

There was something there in his eyes that I couldn't quiet identify. Anger about the topic of conversation, sure, but also maybe a hint of possessiveness, and I liked seeing it. He was entirely different from Jake, who was arrogant and a loose cannon.

"He the one who broke it off?" he asked, his jaw ticking.

"No," I said, sitting back and getting comfortable in the bed. I wanted to pull him to me, but I could tell he was keeping his distance. Like he didn't know what to make of this. So I figured I should give him the whole story and allow him to decide some things for himself. "He was really into me. He's also the person who administered my first shot of heroin. Talked me into it. But in the end, I've got no one to blame but myself."

"Sounds like a real winner," he said, not even attempting to keep the sarcasm out of his voice.

I nodded. "It was the beginning of the end for me. I think he liked the sex when I was high."

"Fuck, man," Vaughn said. "That's some crazy shit."

"Yeah," I said, practically shivering from the memory of being so strung out most days I couldn't even function. "By the time Mal rescued me, I was a fucking mess. Not much of a relationship when you're constantly high."

"Is that how you got your nickname?" he asked. "Because I hope to God it's not because of Mitsy's being torched."

"No, not Mitsy's." I looked grimly at him. "At first, it was because of drag racing. You know, down that strip by the docks? I would smoke all my friends away on my first bike. Back in the day when my dad was still alive and life was pretty simple. Pretty good. But then later…smoked weed at first…then tried heroin…just stuck, I guess…"

I let the sentence hang there so he could fill in the blanks himself.

"I can see how messed up that would be," he said, and he sloped his body toward mine, as if he needed that closeness as much as I did. Maybe he was jealous. Of a man I wanted no part of any longer. Just the thought of being with Jake made me want to hurl.

"That why you're always chomping on that damn gum?" he asked.

I nodded. "Habit I picked up in rehab. That bother you?"

"Nah, it kinda fits. Besides, I like the taste of cinnamon."

He lay down in my arms, and I pulled his warm body flush against mine. It felt so fucking good, I figured I'd keep him wrapped up for as long as I could and then I'd always have the memory to play back in my head.

"Leave it to my pop to get your real name out of you," he said after a while, probably still thinking about how I'd earned that nickname. "But I dig it."

"Yeah?" I said. "Did you almost call it out while I was fucking you?"

He kissed my shoulder. "Would you have wanted that?"

A shiver ran through me. "Maybe."

He tapped our lips—once, twice—before I pulled his mouth to mine, needing something, anything from him. We kissed and nuzzled for long minutes, our tongues lazily rubbing against each other, our hands searching and gripping.

"So what does all of this have to do with me?" he asked, settling back down against me. "Why would Jake ransack my place and leave his fucking *mark*, as you called it?"

I gave him a furtive look, hoping he figured it out on his own.

It was as if a light bulb had gone on over his head. His eyes widened, and he jerked away from me. "So he's been checking up on you, and he thinks you and I are…oh hell."

"Well, we are, aren't we?" I said, raising my eyebrows. "He's not stupid. And if he figured it out, eventually others might, too. Not sure why else he'd bother you."

"Fucking great," he said through clenched teeth. "I haven't been laid by a decent guy in forever and when I finally am…"

"You can't even keep it private. No kidding," I said, finishing his thought. "I feel like shit that I brought this on you. Jake's not a guy you want in your business."

"Hey, man," he said, finally touching me again. His fingers wrapped around my nape, and I practically wilted into his embrace. "It's okay. Not your fault."

"It's absolutely my fault," I said, my lips moving to his neck. "Goddamn it."

I found myself unwinding simply from having him near. When his fingers pushed through my hair, all of the coiled tension inside of me began seeping out. Replaced by a deep thrumming in my gut.

"I haven't screwed around with a guy since Jake, and if he's been watching me…" I took a deep breath and squashed down my anxiety. "Thing is, he might get jealous over the ladies, but he knows I love being with men."

"Is that so?" Vaughn smirked, his length hardening against my thigh.

"Yeah." I smiled sheepishly. "I just, *fuck*…or maybe it's just you. You and all of that charm you've got, reeling me right in."

"I know the feeling." He smiled into the crook of his arm, looking like a younger version of himself. Then he cleared his throat as he remembered the seriousness of the situation.

"So, he knows what you've been up to with the Scorpions?"

It was the one sticking point in my mind. "Not sure."

And then the bigger thought I wasn't certain I should even share aloud came tumbling out. Being around him made me feel like he'd keep my secrets. "Hope I'm not being double-crossed."

His head sprang up, dozens of questions in his eyes.

I shook my head, not willing to share any further. I didn't want him to know that I watched my back when I was with the Scorpions club even though Fish was real tight with Mal.

"Think you should tell the prez?" he asked.

"Fuck, I don't know," I said. "No way I need him catching wind of my private life. He won't be too cool with it. And hell, this is the first time I feel…"

"Feel what?" Vaughn asked, now rubbing his fingers over my thigh, not realizing how much I craved that contact from him.

"Like maybe I belong somewhere," I said, shutting my eyes. "Those guys are my family. More so than any family I've had. I mean, even my dad had his demons. Worked himself to the bone. And my uncle, he…we haven't spoken in years."

I felt the heat from Vaughn's lips as they hovered above me, but I kept my lids closed. He kissed my cheek and then moved across my jaw. "Even if you gotta stay in the closet about liking sex with men?"

"That part never fits, but the rest…yeah," I mumbled as he sucked on the skin right beneath my ear.

I wouldn't tell him that I also felt like *he* fit, which was totally contradictory to what I had said.

Hands gripping his hair, I groaned, tangling my legs with his, my erection poking at his stomach.

"Are you out to your dad?" I whispered.

"Nah. But I guess I never had any good reason before." It seemed like there was more that he wanted to say, but he held himself back. So I waited him out, nearly desperate to know more.

"The last man I'd been with regularly had been an investor in my bar. Before the Disciples became involved," he said. "I should've known better. We were so different."

"Different how?"

"That what's he did for a living. Investing in shit. Had loads of money," he said, and my chest tightened because I had nothing to show for myself. Only my patch and my sobriety. "He knew my dream was to own a bar, and I think he offered to front me the last of the money because he enjoyed fucking me. It wasn't like we were building something together. Wasn't that deep, really."

I tightened my arms around him. "So what happened?"

"He found somebody he liked fucking better. Even moved out of state for him." He sighed. "I got pissed. Dude was cheating on me, said he'd been doing it for weeks."

"Shit," I said. "That's messed up."

"He acted all offended that I was mad, pulled out of the bar business, practically left me stranded." He huffed out a breath. "If it wasn't for Mal stepping in with his idea, I probably would've gone belly up."

"Looks like Mal had a hand in saving the both of us."

"Fuck," he said, barking out an incredulous laugh. "Guess so."

My fingers trailed up and down his back, feeling every smooth plane. "I need to find out some things first before I tell Mal anything."

"So we probably shouldn't…" He trailed off, and my stomach clenched. "I don't want to make any trouble for you…or me, for that matter."

"No way you need to be involved in my shit," I said, trying to keep the disappointment out of my voice. Even though I knew this thing between Vaughn and me was time-limited. I was supposed to get him out of my system, not get caught up in him even further. "I need to keep you out of it."

"Yeah…" he said, the same hesitant look in his eyes. "But…what we just did…was it good for you?"

"Hell yes," I said, grabbing his face and kissing him hard. "More than good. Incredible."

His fingers curled around my neck and then he was kissing me, his tongue invading my mouth. I got so lost in the way his lips felt that I wished we had more time together. Never had someone had this effect on me. It was like every time his skin was next to mine, I lost my train of thought. Disappeared inside him. I couldn't get enough.

"How about you?" I asked, dragging my lips away. "Did you… you know…?"

"Pretty sure I won't forget you fucking me for a good long while."

My heart squeezed so goddamn tight I nearly gasped out loud.

Right then I heard the automatic garage door. Felix was home. Pretty soon his boots would be clomping up the wooden steps to the back entrance. Vaughn remained quiet, listening as well. When I heard the heavy door shut behind Felix, I relaxed and turned back to Vaughn.

"Guess we should…" he said, hesitating. "Hell. Before the shit that went down tonight, I was hoping maybe…"

"Maybe what?" I held my breath.

He kissed my shoulder. "I thought maybe we could've seen each other on the down low every now and again. But that idea doesn't look promising."

I smiled sadly, because I had been wondering the same thing. "Mal is probably gonna have everybody's eyes on you. If it's not me watching over you, it'll be someone else, so that's going to make it a bust, anyway."

"Yeah." He sighed in resignation and then pushed back the sheets. "Should get some sleep."

"Or we can go at it again while we've got the chance." I was tired as hell, but I still wanted him. God, I wanted him.

"Fuck yeah," he said, grinning and then twisting his head into the pillow. "How thin are your walls?"

"Not too bad," I said, thinking of how few times I'd been able to hear Felix banging some chick downstairs. "Let's give it a couple of minutes. He usually turns on music. Says it helps him sleep."

CHAPTER FIFTEEN
VAUGHN

I must've nodded off, because the next thing I felt was my hard-as-nails cock surrounded in wetness and warmth. I heard shallow breaths and an erotic murmur that could only be coming from the one man who got me entirely too worked up.

I opened one eye, and a tangle of blond hair came into view. I glanced down the length of his body, imagining what we must've looked like together. Smoke's back muscles straining, his firm ass slightly lifted in the air, his mouth bobbing up and down between my legs.

His tongue was circling the underside of my cock as he took me all the way to the back of his throat, my girth stretching his lips wide. My hips began swaying toward his mouth as if they had a mind of their own.

"Mmmm…" I murmured in a groggy, lust-laden voice. "What did I do to deserve this?"

"We had unfinished business," he said as his lips suctioned the crown, licking underneath, exactly the way I loved. I gripped a handful of hair and groaned. "You zonked out on me, old man."

"I ain't got that many years on you. Six, maybe?" I huffed out as his thumb circled my balls. "So you felt the need to wake me up?'

"Oh yeah. Couldn't help myself." I felt the vibration of his voice on my skin as needy pinpricks of heat licked at my lower spine. "This cock is perfection. So damn thick I can barely fit the entire thing in my mouth."

I wanted to make a crack about fitting it in his ass, but that was a subject that wasn't up for discussion. Besides, I could barely think straight with his mouth and lips and tongue expertly blowing me. His fingers added extra pressure to my sac. In another minute I was going to come, and I wasn't ready for this to end.

"You gonna fuck me again?" I panted openly and grabbed more firmly onto his hair, tightening my fist around it.

He pulled my cock out of his mouth but still held my dick in his hand, stroking with a firm grip. "You want me inside you again?"

"Please," I said, pumping into his fist as his fingers reached down to his own engorged cock, his hungry gaze sliding up to mine. I couldn't help feeling smug that he was already so hard for me.

"You think he'll hear us downstairs?"

"His bedroom is on the opposite side." He smirked. "Like I said last night, he sleeps with music on."

I strained my ears. "I think I can hear it. That horrible 80s shit."

"Next time ask him to change the station." He laughed and then sobered as if remembering there wouldn't be a next time.

"Let me turn over," I said, attempting to lift up and out of his grasp.

"No," he said, laying a kiss on my collarbone. "Stay just how you are."

I sank back down and yanked his mouth toward mine, my tongue tangling powerfully with his. The kiss was deep and lingering and so intense it felt like it might be our last. I thrust the thought aside. If he wanted to fuck one final time, I needed to savor all of this. His taste, his spicy smell, his sexy noises.

Our slick cocks were rubbing between us, and I was already so close from his mouth being on me that the friction alone would send me over the edge.

"Fuck me," I said in a hoarse voice, brushing my lips against his.

He reached for lube and a condom in his bedside drawer, which momentarily reminded me of the mess that had been strewn across my bed last night, and my stomach nearly revolted. Smoke seemed to know almost instinctually what I was feeling, and he grabbed my face and kissed me so hard, my thoughts vacated my brain. All I was left with was sensation.

"I want to be inside you so bad," he said as his finger slipped beneath my balls and pressed against my ring of muscle. I tensed briefly before opening my legs wider to allow him better access. I groaned and pumped against him as he slid a second finger alongside the first. He thrust a few times and then curved them upward, finding that perfect spot inside that instantly turned my limbs to mush.

"Uuuhhh," I said as my cock hardened even further. The pleasure receptors inside my brain went haywire, and my eyes slid shut while he continued to indulge me. "I need you. Now."

He lined up his dick with my hole, and we both groaned as he pressed inside.

"Oh fuck fuck fuck," Smoke chanted, and then he inhaled deeply through his nose. "You feel so damn good."

This position was so much more intimate because the way he was staring into my eyes was nearly my undoing. Facing away from him before, I could get lost in the moment. But watching him get his pleasure—take it from me—made me wish we could screw in his bed anytime we wanted. And that was such a dangerous wish.

He drove in more forcefully, his hands clutching my thighs, his balls slapping against my ass.

"God, yes," I slurred, watching how a flush crawled up his chest to his neck and face. He was straining, drenched with sweat, and toeing the line of his orgasm. I allowed him to take me to the precipice time and again until I was damp and begging for it. He grasped my cock and pumped me until I was muttering senselessly.

"Uhhhh, Reed!" I called out his given name without any forethought. I shuddered violently as spurts of come burst over my chest and neck, some of it landing on my chin.

His eyes widened in wonder, and I considered whether I'd just ruined it all until his gaze deepened with passion and something else I couldn't name.

He bent over and licked the come off my neck, then traced the outline of my lips so that I could taste myself on him. I threw back my head and groaned against the pillow.

"Goddamn, Vaughn. So fucking sexy." His thighs began quivering as he drove inside me like a man on a mission. His movements became labored and uninspired right before his eyes rolled back in his head and he came so hard, his teeth practically clattered.

* * *

We had fallen asleep from sheer exhaustion. By the time I woke up a couple of hours later, the rays of sunlight through the window were already bright and blinding. The bed was empty beside me, and I couldn't say I wasn't disappointed.

Last night with Smoke had been amazing. I wasn't sure what would even compare. But I couldn't spend any more minutes thinking about that. I needed to compartmentalize this time with him in my brain and get the hell on with it.

I pulled on my jeans and shoved my fingers through my messy hair. When I entered the kitchen, Smoke was standing over the sink in only his sweats, pouring a cup of java.

He looked back at me. "How do you take yours?"

"Black." It would've felt pretty nice and domestic to have him serve me coffee if there wasn't a sense of anxiety and gloom hanging over us this morning.

He reached for a cup and began pouring. I was tempted to sidle up behind him and kiss his skin—his shoulder or his neck—but somehow the harshness of reality made me reconsider. Besides, after we had laid it all out last night, this had been only a hookup, and we needed to be careful now because of his suspicions about the other club.

He handed me the mug, and as I took a big swig, I noticed how his eyes scrolled down my body, checking me out in the daylight.

"You like what you see?" I asked with a smirk.

"More than," he said, and then slurped at the brown liquid in his cup.

"You're not too bad yourself," I said, and then turned away to search for my keys on his coffee table so that my hardening cock wouldn't betray me.

"Want some toast or cereal or something?" He looked so earnest that it made me want to pull out a chair and plop down, but we both knew I had already overstayed my welcome.

"Nah, it's cool. I rarely eat breakfast anyway," I said, taking another grateful swig. "Besides, we slept late. Better hit the road and get my place back in order."

"Our cleaning crew has already been to your apartment," he said, motioning to his phone lying on the counter. Maybe he'd gotten a call from Mal and that was what had woken him up.

A wash of relief swept through me that I wouldn't have to walk back into my place with it looking how it did last night. "Thanks, man."

"No problem," he said. "Least I could do after…"

I held up my hand. "No need to say it."

I went back to his room, pulled on my shirt, grabbed my wallet, and used the restroom.

As I made my way to the door, my eyes met his, and I saw something in his gaze. Something that made me pause. Worry, melancholy, affection.

"You see anything suspicious, you let me know," he said.

"What does Jake look like?" I asked tentatively. "Just curious…need to know who I'm dealing with."

He nodded once. "Brown hair, usually wears it longer, ties it behind his bandana. Skinnier than you."

My stomach squeezed, but I played it off with a smirk. "You like them thin, huh?"

He looked me up and down, making gooseflesh break out. "I like them just like you."

"Good to know." I turned the knob before I did something else to prolong my visit. "Catch you later."

All of a sudden, fingers curled over the top of my hand and he flung me around, forcing my shoulders against the door.

"What the hell are you doing?" I said as my breath swept out of my lungs at the intensity of his gaze.

"Getting one last taste," he growled, forcing his groin against mine. "Not sure if I'll be able to again."

He grabbed my neck and crushed his mouth against mine, nudging my lips apart. His tongue delved deep as it explored all the crooks and angles of my mouth. He kissed and nipped and licked me into submission, making certain to swipe at the scar on my lower lip, which he seemed so mesmerized by. I was a quivering mess before he released me and let me walk out the door.

That kiss was something. It was as if he had marked my soul.

As I bounded down the stairs, my hands shaky on the railing, the hairs stood up on the back of my neck. I got this strange sensation that even though we probably had a snowball's chance in hell to ever be a real couple, something might happen to forever guarantee it.

Chapter Sixteen
Vaughn

Between the intense makeout session and the eerie sense of doom, I could barely see straight enough to drive home. Thankfully I hadn't spotted Felix on the way out, and hopefully he hadn't heard Smoke fucking me that last time. At least I wouldn't be showing up there again, so even if he had caught wind of something, it could easily be explained away.

By the time I got to my apartment building I already felt different. Changed. Almost like this place didn't belong to me anymore, and that pissed me off. I'd been renting this unit for the better part of five years. Maybe it wasn't the best place I'd ever lived, but I had done what I could to make it my home.

That motherfucker Jake had better leave me the hell alone. He tries anything again, hopefully I'll be waiting for him and his skinny ass.

I could smell the disinfectant as soon as the key turned in the lock. As I walked through the rooms, I saw how shiny all the surfaces were. When I got to my bedroom, no evidence of what had gone down was in sight, and I breathed a sigh of relief.

The aroma of urine had been completely obliterated, and now that the contents littering my bed had been cleared, I gathered up my comforter and sheets and walked out to the laundry room to throw them into a hot water cycle. I overloaded the detergent for sure and even considered throwing them in the garbage bin, but I figured this was a decent start.

Then I pulled a second sheet set out of the linen closet and made the bed. I finally felt clean and allowed myself to breathe deeply as I sat down hard on the edge.

Over the years I had never asked for anything from the Disciples.

I enjoyed owning the Hog's Den and doing my job. I was a simple man, much like my father.

The Disciples had some bad stuff go down in years past at the bar, mostly meetings that had gotten out of hand as Mal continued to clean up his father's past sins. But nobody had every come into my home and messed with me.

Had Smoke never said anything about his suspicions, I would have gone on assuming it was some sick fuck who was a former patron of the bar. Maybe somebody I had kicked out. But now I couldn't help thinking one or both of us was in danger.

It could've happened sooner given my association with the club, but didn't it just figure it was related to some of the most satisfying sex of my life.

And until we figured this one out, we'd have to go on pretending that we weren't doing anything on the side. Of course we were already pretending. But that was in front of the Disciples. Not to be able to take your private business home with you was a different story.

I took a quick shower and got ready to open the bar. I called my dad to check on him, leaving out the details of my break-in. No reason for him to worry.

When I pulled in the lot, I spotted other bikes, which meant early club business. Two of the Disciples had some short guy with a large gut out by the back dumpster.

"I catch you coming around here again," Jonas was saying, and I averted my gaze as he finished his intimidation of the guy, whom I didn't recognize. More than likely he was some small-time criminal who had crossed their path. "This is our turf."

I'd seen plenty over the years, so that kind of scene didn't even make me flinch. But this time I made sure to catalogue the guy's face for future reference. I didn't know what was going to come at me next.

It also afforded me the sobering realization of why Smoke was anxious about crossing his brothers. We might have been cool with each other, but this was still an outlaw motorcycle club. Sure, they were pulling themselves out of some messes, but they looked the other way when those parts came into their shop. They'd take you down if they had to, no question.

I heard Mal's voice in the back room as I quietly strode to my office. I had some paperwork to catch up on before I took stock of the bar. As I twisted the knob, I heard another deep and familiar voice. Mal was speaking to Smoke, and before I could step inside the room I heard him say, "You keep eyes on Vaughn every night."

"Maybe that's not a good idea," Smoke said in a strangled voice, and I tensed up. "I already do that here. Maybe one of the other recruits—"

"You got a problem with Vaughn?" Mal's voice boomed, and I could tell he was irritated with Smoke back-talking him. Fortunately I understood why Smoke was trying to stay away.

"No at all, but what if—"

"What if *what*?" Mal asked.

Shit, he had him trapped.

"Nothing, Prez." I couldn't tell if Smoke was standing or seated, but I could picture his head bowed down in deference to the one man he respected beyond all others in this organization.

Mal smacked his hand on the desk and I jumped. "You got too many jobs, too much to do?"

"No, Prez." Smoke's voice was tight, quiet. As if he were getting a lecture from a parent figure. And maybe that's what Mal had come to represent to him.

"You don't trust my instincts on this?" Mal said through clenched teeth.

"That's not it," Smoke said in quick succession.

"So when I give you a direct order, I don't want any protest unless it's real important." I heard the scraping of a chair and imagined Mal standing up suddenly. "And so far you've given me nothing."

I heard Smoke sigh in defeat. "Sure, I got him covered, Mal."

I hurried into my office and sat down at my desk. I was lucky nobody had caught me eavesdropping. I didn't do shit like that. Normally I heard enough to have a general idea of club business. But this time it concerned me, and I couldn't help listening.

Unexpectedly, Smoke was standing in the doorway, and even though I was pretending to be busy, it was no use. He looked behind him before stepping inside and shutting the door.

"You heard that?" he asked, biting his lip.

I leaned back in my chair, spreading my legs wide, and Smoke followed my motion. "Yeah."

He took a step forward. "You understand why I—"

I held up my hand to stop him. "Of course." But there was a small tremor in my voice.

Just drinking in the sight of him made my balls tingle in response. The idea of being with somebody else after Smoke made my stomach bottom out. I was beginning feel a bit frazzled and consumed. What the hell had I gotten myself into?

Simply standing this distance from him now, getting the faint whiff of his spicy cinnamon scent, made me feel so animalistic, I wanted to pull him over the desk and claim him as mine.

But he wasn't mine. He would never be mine. Not in the way I was beginning to want him to be. And that was pretty fucked up, because I had no idea what the man in front of me was truly feeling beyond his all-encompassing desire for me. That much was obvious. But that was also purely sexual. We were definitely good in bed together.

"Listen," Smoke said so low I almost didn't hear him. "You're going to have to pretend, man. Just business as usual."

"Sure, of course." I cocked my head to the side. "How do you mean?"

He looked at the ground, not meeting my eyes. "Bring some girl home this week. So Jake thinks…"

So that Jake would think he was wrong about the two of us. As evidenced by the fact that Smoke couldn't even get the words out, he wouldn't be wrong at all. I'd admit I liked hearing him struggle. It meant I wasn't alone in this. "I'll try my best."

There was something in his gaze he was fighting. He knew damn well I didn't want to bring home anybody else. And he didn't want me to, either. But this was the way things had to be. Still, it would've been nice to hear it voiced out loud.

"I'll keep patrol with Felix," he said. "See if we come up with anything."

"Think that'll do it?" I said. "Pretend we're not together. That we were never together. Go about my business?"

"Unless the fucker had binoculars and saw inside your place…" He finally looked at me, and there was sadness and resignation in his eyes. Also a good dose of uncertainty, like he knew what this guy was capable of. "It's worth a shot."

CHAPTER SEVENTEEN
SMOKE

Fuck, I had brought this on myself. I allowed myself a taste of Vaughn, and now look at the mess I was in. If my suspicions were right, Jake had been keeping tabs on me and was trying to fuck with Vaughn.

But damn, now Vaughn was all I could think about. His tongue inside my mouth, his throaty moans when I thrust inside him. But those memories would have to do, because shit was going down and I didn't have a good feeling about it. At all.

I headed to the Scorpions compound to meet up with Fish and his crew. I felt terrible hiding things from Mal. But I needed to figure some things out on my own first. Get my head on straight. Maybe this thing with Vaughn was scrambling my brain.

I parked outside the large concrete structure, which looked like it might've been an old school building taken over by a bunch of bikers. Uneasiness settled in my stomach, not because I was fearful of being here. But because I was about to give up some intel on my old club. And I was uncertain of exactly who was screwing with me.

Some of Fish's crew, who were playing pool in the large and spacious room, nodded in my direction. Another guy by the door told me that Fish was waiting in the back room.

One of his men looked up from his smartphone and seemed to follow my every move. When my gaze met his, he looked me up and down in a way that made me uncomfortable. Not because he was being cautious or protective.

That would've been easier to understand. The look was one of lust, like he was checking me out. But that couldn't be right. I was probably reading too much into it. Regardless, it was awkward, so I averted my gaze and kept on walking. But I could still feel him gawking at my ass.

Fish was sitting with a couple of his men at a smaller round table, poring over something on his computer screen.

Fish stood and shook my hand, as did his two men. "Have a seat, Smoke."

He turned the monitor toward me and clicked through a series of photos.

"This is out at the Russian warehouse. It looks like the Asylum was casing the joint." It showed the men dressed in black climbing in through a window and apparently having a look around.

I pointed to the screen. "That's Johnny and a guy they call Horse."

One of his guys snorted. "As in hung?"

"Something like that," I said grimly, remembering how many women that guy had been with. "He was pretty proud of it."

Fish's voice was harsh as he attempted to rein us back in. "So these fuckers are trying to skim off the top, even though they've got a deal in the works with the Latino mob?"

I shrugged, because I wasn't going to presume the wrong thing. Not all of those guys were bad news. Some were only lost like I had been, and I would have hated to see them taken out.

"I know they wanted the Russian territory pretty badly because of the location and because the police chief in that district looks the other way," I said. "Plus Terrence hates the Russians because of some old beef with them."

"Enough to stage a break-in or a takedown?" he asked. "We need to give them a heads-up if our intel is right. And then we can have an ally when we bring them down."

I cringed. Fuck, an all-out war was what they were setting up.

"The situation might've changed since I was with them, but I do remember one thing," I said, making sure my voice didn't waver. "When Terrence gets it in his head that somebody has done him wrong, he's tough to reason with, for sure."

Fish stared at me long and hard, and I nearly faltered beneath his gaze, but I held my ground. "Thanks for your insight."

I sure hoped that Mal knew what he was doing by asking me to help them out.

But I trusted him, didn't I? Wasn't that why I had sworn allegiance again to another club? Maybe it was the Scorpions club that I didn't trust. But unless I told Mal my suspicions, how was he to know how I felt? Maybe he was relying on me to tell him just that.

I headed to the auto parts store to report to Mal. When I got there, Felix informed me that he had just left to meet with Jonas at the Hog's Den.

"That a new shipment?"

Felix nodded as he signed the driver's form and then opened the doors to unload. We didn't ask where the dealer got the parts he supplied to our shop, but he charged a fair price and kept us in a lucrative business.

"Is my piece ready to be fired back there?" I asked. Felix was busy helping the driver unload one of the large boxes.

"All set," he said, looking back at me. "That is a thing of beauty. The customer is going to love it. I almost want to keep it for myself."

I nodded, pride blooming in my chest. I headed back to my creation, which was my version of a knight on horseback. I had used hubcaps to create the mare's flank and chest and then smaller scrap pieces that I had heated and manipulated to form the mane.

For the next hour I got lost in my work, which helped relieve the tension from my meeting with Fish.

"All set," I said to Felix as I wiped my hands on a clean towel. He was bent over a shelf of belts and hoses, adjusting the sales price. "The customer can pick it up in twenty-four hours. Needs drying time."

Then I headed to the Hog's Den. When I came through the back door, my gaze immediately sought out Vaughn's. It was a slower night, but I couldn't help wanting to be behind the bar with him, to be part of something more solid, rather than that slippery meeting I was just involved in with the Scorpions.

Sure, we'd dealt with way worse, but with Mal trying to clean up the club, this felt like taking a step backward.

When Vaughn met my gaze, he tipped his chin. The woman in front of him was attempting to gain his attention, and when he threw her his trademark killer smile, my heart knocked hard against my chest. As he quickly glanced up at me and then back to her, I knew what his play was going to be.

He held steady to his rule of never dating customers, so I knew this was about my plan to get Jake off his back. Still, my heart had climbed a thorny path to my throat.

Turning away, I told myself this was how it needed to be.

I found Mal at the back table with Jonas. "Grab a seat," Mal said.

I sat backward on the chair with my eyes to the front, so I could steal glances at the bar and watch Vaughn work his magic. Pure torture.

It was interesting viewing Vaughn from this vantage point, because he was always moving, speaking, grinning, and joking around. He was in his element here, and it showed. The only time I saw different was when he was out at the compound or when we were behind closed doors.

Sure, he liked to talk while I was giving it to him good, but he was needy and demanding and nearly desperate at times. Writhing and grinding and moaning. Fuck, I loved that side of him. The one that sounded so wrecked for me.

"How did your meeting go with Fish?" Mal asked, bringing me out of my thoughts. I needed to get my shit together.

"Fine," I said, and it only took a split second before he heard the hesitation in my voice.

He grasped at my shoulder. "What is it, Smoke?"

"I…" I looked into his eyes and saw concern there. "I don't know, man."

"What is it with you lately?" he grunted out. "You got something to say, you better say it, before it's too late."

I looked back and forth between him and Jonas. "I'm afraid that what Fish has planned will bring us back in the mix, and other clubs will want retaliation."

Mal's eyebrows scrunched together. "Go on."

"I know this is paying back a final debt," I said, choosing my words carefully. "But I don't know…I've kind of got a bad feeling about this."

"Bad how?" Jonas asked, his brows arching behind his messy bangs. "You don't think Fish is on the up and up?"

I thought about it for a long, hard minute.

"I know you told me you and Fish go way back," I said. "But I wonder if he'll only think of his club when it comes down to it. If he'll throw us under the bus."

As Mal stared at me, I squirmed. Then something gave way in his gaze. A moment of respect. He clapped me on the back. "I told Jonas you would be our man."

"What do you mean?"

"That you've got a good head, that you'd tell us if something felt off." His gaze cut briefly to Jonas. "That's why I needed you on this and nobody else. Sure, this is personal for you, but it's not clouding your brain. You're still thinking straight, still got our back."

"Okay," I said, nearly wincing. I wasn't sure that I deserved his accolade.

"For the record, I do trust Fish. He's done me plenty of favors," he said. "But keep your eyes open. You tell me if you see something that double-crosses us."

I hesitated, almost told him about Jake and me, but that was about sex and jealousy, right? Not club business. Not yet. One more day. "Will do."

I hung around with the guys and played a round of darts until almost closing time. Because Mal was insisting that I keep eyes on Vaughn, I was headed out on patrol tonight with Felix.

The same woman Vaughn had been flirting with earlier had remained at the bar all night, and I knew he'd be taking her home. Against Vaughn's own rule. In order to straighten out everything that was fucked up. Except what he and I had done didn't feel wrong—not when it had been that good.

What was wrong was that somebody cared enough to mess with us. My gut tightened as I avoided eye contact with him. I didn't want him to see my hesitation as I made my way toward the exit.

An hour later, after I had patrolled up and down the west end, I met up with Felix, and we made a swing near Vaughn's place.

"Looks like Vaughn is getting some action tonight," Felix said as we watched Vaughn pull into his lot with the woman from the bar on the back of his hog.

My throat struggled to work past the grit firmly lodged there. "Guess so."

I watched for far too long after they headed inside. I imagined his lips on hers, his face as he got his release. My fingers tightened on the handlebars. For Vaughn's benefit, I gunned my engine like some fucking adolescent, to alert him that I was there.

Before I could further give myself away to Felix, I drove the hell out of there.

CHAPTER EIGHTEEN
SMOKE

It was a Wednesday night at the compound and not much was going on, but Mal wanted to have a little celebration for Jonas's birthday. So all the usual suspects had shown up for some grilling and keg drinking.

This party was pretty tame in comparison to some I'd been to in the past, and I was beginning to wonder if the club was slowing down, becoming more grounded. One of the old ladies had even baked a slew of cupcakes that were calling to me across the room. Sure, there was still a fair number of single men and women in attendance here, but nobody was taking off their clothes in the middle of the room. Yet.

I'd been able to keep my distance from Vaughn the last couple of nights. I'd seen him only when I was on patrol, as he made his way home from the bar, alone except for that first night. I hoped that meant he wasn't all that into bringing somebody else to his place, though I shouldn't have been feeling that way. He had done it to keep Jake off his back.

I hadn't been able to ask Vaughn about our plan, because we had too many eyes on us at the bar. I wasn't scheduled to work with him until tomorrow night, and the time away did little to clear my head.

So when I made my way toward the back patio where the cooler of drinks was located, I nearly swallowed my own tongue at seeing Vaughn shooting the breeze with Jonas. Not only because Mal liked to get on his case about not attending a Disciples party in months, but because Wednesday was the only day of the week he got the night off.

The bar was closed and I figured he had plenty of other things to do with his time, so maybe Mal had talked him into coming. Or maybe Vaughn was showing his thanks for the help on his burglary.

I reached for a soda, my heart rate skyrocketing at seeing him in this environment. I needed to keep my head, so I schooled my features and clapped him on the back. "Strange not seeing you behind that bar."

"That's what I told him, " Jonas said from beside him, as Vaughn attempted not to make direct eye contact with me. Maybe he was having the same difficulty. "Glad he could finally join us out here. It's been a while."

He shot me a look out of the corner of his eye, because we both knew exactly when that last time had been. Fuck, I tried to think of anything else besides the way he looked naked.

When Jonas got caught up in a side conversation with one of the recruits, I muttered, "Did Mal twist your arm to get you out here?"

"Not exactly," he said, his lips a grim line. "Honestly, it's been weird being at my place since the break-in."

"Fuck. Sorry about that, " I said, not really considering he'd be feeling that way. Come to think of it, it did look like there were dark circles forming beneath his eyes. Was he not sleeping at night? I wished he'd have let me know. "You're free to crash in one of the spare bedrooms here."

I wanted to suggest sleeping at my place, but we both knew that was no longer possible.

"Yeah, thanks. I'm not really one to avoid situations, so I'll make my way back to my place eventually," he said, smirking, but it didn't reach his eyes.

"Figured you'd just invite a girl home with you every night."

He stared at me skeptically, and I practically squirmed beneath his gaze. We were playing a game here, and neither of us liked it one bit.

Suddenly there were female hands on him from behind. "You look tense," a compound frequenter named Melanie said.

She used to be Slim's old lady, but they'd broken up a while back. Once you were a regular, though, it was hard to give up the amenities. I think she was hoping to be picked up by another biker, and I guess Vaughn was close enough. She was a good lady, though, and enjoyed partying with the boys and having a good time.

My jaw tightened. "There you go. Somebody to help you get your mind off of it."

It was the plan we had talked about but still, it was tough to watch firsthand. What the hell had I been thinking, getting involved with him to begin with? I had fucked him into my mattress—hell, even my sheets still smelled like him—and now all I wanted was to do it again.

She began massaging his shoulders and he didn't cringe or wave her off, which made my stomach perform some acrobatics routine.

"I'll be patrolling, so it'll be cool," I said, lowering my voice. "You can relax. You know, about being in your place."

He leaned over and whispered in my ear. "Does your patrol include peeking inside the windows?"

I nearly blushed. Did he mean he wanted me to watch *him* or whomever he brought home with him?

"Could be arranged…" I grunted. "If I don't run them off first."

"Why would you do that?" He grasped Melanie's hands, which had been raking over his pecs, and positioned her in front of him. He rubbed her neck and she moaned a little. I kept my face neutral though I was seething inside.

I knew he was only playing the part like I had suggested, but any more contact and I'd have to walk the fuck away. I had never felt jealousy before, not over a woman or man, but it was like she was getting the prize that I so desperately wanted. I nearly sulked like a little kid.

"What are you two up to?" Melanie asked, looking back and forth between us. "Am I about to get a treat from the both of you?"

My eyebrow shot up. A threesome with Vaughn hadn't even crossed my mind. Could be interesting. He seemed to think so as well, as his eyes surveyed me over her shoulder.

She nuzzled his ear, and he seemed to be appreciate the contact. Either that or he was enjoying torturing me again. I couldn't take my eyes off of them. Because fuck, after having him the other night, I didn't want him with anybody else.

I wanted to be the only one to suck his cock. To touch him. Smell him. Kiss that scar below his lip. Make his eyes soften, his mouth go slack, as he pleaded with me to rock his world.

When Melanie leaned forward and kissed Vaughn, he stiffened at first, and then closed his eyes, seeming to throw himself into it. Though I was pissed, my dick actually throbbed in response from seeing how hungry and eager his lips were.

When she got a bit carried away by grabbing the back of his head and nearly straddling him right in the middle of the room, his eyes flew open, and he took a backward step.

"Calm it down, baby," he said in a soothing voice. "How about getting another drink so Smoke and I can discuss what you're proposing?"

I swept her hair behind her ear, and Vaughn visibly tensed. He didn't like it any more than I did. "You sure that's what you want, Melanie?" I asked.

"Is that even a valid question?" she drawled. "You two are hot as fuck. Why wouldn't I want you?"

I knew that plenty of guys here engaged in threesomes, but never had that thought appealed to me until now. Simply being in the same room with Vaughn would be a turn-on.

Vaughn sat down on the couch as she walked away to grab a drink. I sat down beside him. "What the hell are we doing here?"

"Exactly what you proposed, right?" he said with a clenched jaw. "Make sure I look straight as they come."

"Listen, I know this is rough, but I'm only trying—" Before I could finish my thought, Melanie returned and plopped down on Vaughn's knees. She twisted to kiss his neck and wiggle in his lap. My cock plumped up simply from having the heat of his thigh next to mine as he readjusted himself.

When she leaned toward me, my hand clenched her shoulder. "I think it's time to take this somewhere private," I said.

I was never one for public displays of affection, but not being able to touch Vaughn was making me crazy.

Vaughn stared at me, something unreadable in his eyes, while he played with her hair. I cleared my throat. "Head to the last bedroom on the right," I said, "and I'll follow in a couple of minutes."

After they left, I caught Jonas's eye across the room. He lifted his eyebrows as if to say, *You getting in on that action?*

I shrugged, anxiously needing to head back to that room, but not wanting to appear too desperate. Jonas gave me the thumbs-up, and I slowly made my way, eager to be near Vaughn again.

Melanie and Vaughn were lip-locked on the bed, and I realized in that instant it would be pure torture not to be able to kiss Vaughn. This threesome wasn't going to involve any male-on-male action. Sure, we could make her feel good, but I couldn't do the same to Vaughn, not in this situation.

Vaughn must've come to the same realization, because he was silent as I entered the room, his eyes solely focused on me.

"You boys are so sexy," Melanie said, coaxing me to the bed. One knee on the mattress, I leaned over and rubbed my lips against hers. Her tongue felt too delicate and soft in my mouth. God, I was fucked in the head. Vaughn's hand briefly caressed the small of my back, and it made me shiver.

I felt the blush creeping across my neck from one simple stroke of fingers. Melanie must've interpreted it as passion, because she began rubbing both of our erections through our pants. I was only at half mast from being so near Vaughn, so I switched gears and reached for her shirt instead, lifting it over her head.

She moaned, unhooking her own bra and yanking it away from her ample breasts.

"Gorgeous," Vaughn said, reaching out to trace his fingers along one of her nipples, and I mimicked his actions on the other side. She was shivering and already hungry for more, and I felt guilty for even taking part. What in the fuck was wrong with me?

A sexy girl was sitting naked in front of me. She was fun and enjoyed having sex, and I was completely engrossed in the only other guy in the room.

Best I could do was help get her off and then extract myself from this situation.

Vaughn laid her on her back and then sucked on one of her breasts. I dipped my head, and just as I was licking around her nipple, I felt Vaughn's cheek brush against mine. I become motionless when I heard him gulp. It was so hard not to turn my head and move my lips to his chin, his scruff, his mouth. But we both knew there'd be hell to pay for that.

Though this ménage might've seemed private, Melanie most likely would talk to the other biker chicks about what happened in this room. Especially if two men from the club had stroked or kissed.

So instead I changed course and slid my mouth down her stomach to the button of her pants. I decided right then and there that I wasn't going to fuck her. Not tonight. Not ever. I wasn't into her, but I'd play along for a little while longer. I didn't want her to think I wasn't hot for her, because in any other situation I might've been.

Vaughn and I both worked on yanking down her jeans, while she squirmed and moaned. Vaughn thankfully had the wherewithal to dirty-talk her and praise her body, because I had pretty much turned mute.

I couldn't get any words out. I felt so completely confused. My brain was going haywire from being next to him and not being able to touch him.

Melanie reached for me, but I pushed back on the bed.

"No, baby," I said, trying to clear my dry throat. "I want to watch Vaughn finger you."

Her eyes lit up, and she turned her attention to Vaughn. I saw his jaw tick, so I didn't know if he was pissed at my suggestion or having the same struggle as me. Right before his fingers reached her clit, he glanced up at me with such raw intensity, it was like a bolt of lightning had struck in my chest.

His fingers went to work, and I concentrated on watching her face.

She was writhing and fisting the pillow, so I knew he was doing a bang-up job. His hands could make anybody horny. My knee was right next to where Vaughn placed his hand to brace himself on the bed, and his knuckles grazed purposefully against my jeans.

That action only made me uncomfortably hard. It almost felt like his hand was working *my* groin. That's how horny he'd made me from a simple brush of his fingers.

I reached out to tweak Melanie's nipples, helping her sail firmly over the edge. Right as she was catching her breath, telling Vaughn he had magic fingers, and I was thinking of a reason to excuse myself, we heard shouting from the other room.

I jumped up and bolted for the door, wondering what in the hell was happening.

Our new recruit named Simon was being held back by Felix. Looked like he had tried to punch out one of the other guests, who was rubbing his reddened jaw. We'd seen this impulsive behavior from Simon before, and Mal had warned him to curb his drinking or he'd be out on his ass.

Just as Vaughn stepped up behind me, Felix turned and caught my eye. "Simon needs to sleep it off in the back room. A little help here?"

I nodded and grabbed Simon's other arm. We dragged him down the hall to the same bedroom Vaughn and Melanie and I had vacated. I pulled back the comforter, and we pushed him down in bed. The moment his head hit the pillow, he mumbled inaudibly and zonked out.

Felix was breathing heavily from the exertion. "Dumbass. Fighting over a game of pool. Competitive bastard."

"Mal is going have words in the morning, and he'd better hope he doesn't have to pack his bags."

Felix wiped his hands down his pants. "Ready to get the hell out of here and patrol?"

"Right behind you."

When we headed back down the hallway, I spotted Melanie slumped against the arm of the couch, chatting with a couple other ladies. She still looked strung out from Vaughn's voodoo hands. Damn lucky.

As I followed Felix out the door, I nearly ran into Vaughn heading toward the exit at the same time.

"You out of here?" I asked, not wanting him to see the relief that was probably evident on my face.

"More than done for the night," he grumbled.

"Yeah?" I held his gaze for entirely too long, trying to read something there.

"For sure. *Bastard*." He bumped my shoulder a little too aggressively, showing me he was ticked about how everything went down in that bedroom.

Then he threw me that devastating grin that practically liquefied me from the inside.

CHAPTER NINETEEN
VAUGHN

"Okay, Pop, if you need anything, you know where to find me," I said, backing out the door. I ignored the feeling in my gut that told me he wasn't looking so well. Ever since that day I drove him to the cemetery, he'd seemed more quiet and reserved.

I sat with him a few nights ago and pretended to watch his favorite show with interest, even asking him questions about the antiques he seemed most engrossed with. Short of moving him into my apartment, which he would never go for, I tried my best to spend more time with him while nudging him to be more active.

I had even offered to stay with him for a while, since my apartment was feeling especially foreign anyway, but he wanted nothing to do with it. He hated being coddled, and I didn't want him to feel like less of a man.

Cherry was already at the Hog's Den when I arrived. She usually showed up early to help set up. When Smoke emerged from the back room with a tray of freshly washed bar glasses, my pulse throbbed unsteadily. The last time I'd seen him, I had my fingers inside a woman's pussy. Smoke had encouraged the play without partaking in it himself, and I had felt pissed and a bit numb afterward. Thoroughly confused over my feelings about Smoke.

"How's your dad doing?" Cherry asked. "It was nice to see him the other night."

I jerked my shoulder. "I don't know if he'd actually admit anything to me if he was feeling lousy."

"Same as my mom," she said, refilling the napkin holders. "They just don't want us to worry."

"Exactly," I said. "I wish he'd just follow the damn doctor's orders about exercise."

"How about your folks, Smoke?" she asked, attempting to include him in the conversation. She didn't realize it was the wrong thing to ask.

But he recovered well. "My mom died when I was young. But my dad used to be the same way, before he also...you know..."

"Shit. I'm sorry, honey," she said, knocking her palm against her forehead. "I didn't know."

"No big thing," he said. Then he picked up an empty box. "I'll get more longnecks from the back room."

When he left, Cherry looked at me regretfully.

"Just trying to get to know him better," she mumbled. "He helps out here and is a hard worker. But don't seem to know anything else about him."

I nodded. "Always been quiet. Might take time."

"He seems to be okay with you."

I stiffened. "What do you mean?"

"Only that there's an ease between the two of you," she said. "Seems like he enjoys working behind that bar."

"His family used to own Mitsy's." My shoulders unwound. "So he's used to this kind of environment."

"Mitsy's," she said, attempting to jog her memory. "Sounds familiar."

I inspected the juices on the lower shelf. "There was a fire and his dad died in the blaze."

"Shit," she said, her hands clutching her hips. "I remember that fire."

I stood up and grabbed another empty box from beneath the shelf. I headed toward the back room, not really considering the consequences, just wanting to be near Smoke. Fuck, even the thought of not being able to touch him again made my fingers itch.

I slipped inside, closing the door behind me. He was down on one knee, taking stock of the beer that'd just been delivered yesterday.

"What's up?" he asked without looking up. His voice sounded different, almost tentative. Call it my imagination, but maybe our feelings weren't mutual. Maybe I hadn't sensed the same hesitation in that bedroom with Melanie. But I sure needed to find out.

"Hey," I said, trying to find the words. "What happened last night? You seemed…"

He stopped shuffling bottles around. "I don't know. Not my thing."

I crossed my arms over my chest and looked back to be sure I had indeed shut the door. "You gonna be honest with me or what?"

He shrugged. "No fun if I don't get to touch you in the process."

My body went lax and I bit back a groan. "Was thinking the same thing."

He looked up at me for the first time, his eyes penetrating, his lips pink and inviting. "Oh yeah?"

"Fuck yeah," I said, my frustrating seeping out. "You're all I can think about anymore."

He stood. "You've been with two hot girls in one week."

I stalked toward him. "You thought I wanted to be with them? Or was I only following your plan?"

He took a step back as if still uncertain. "But you like women."

"So do you." My voice was tight, challenging. I wanted to pull him into a scorching kiss. Right then and there.

"What's your point?" he asked, holding my gaze.

"You only wanted to watch when you could've gotten your rocks off."

"Changed my mind." He huffed out a breath. "She was not the person I was dying to be with."

My hand reached for his hip as I stepped into his space. I could feel him tremble. "And who were you dying to be with?"

He averted his gaze. "You know who."

My lips moved toward his ear. "I'd still like to hear you say it."

"Fuck," he grumbled. "You, okay? I think about my tongue in your mouth. My cock in your ass."

"I think about those things too, you know," I said. "Day and night."

His throat released a whimper as his fingers grasped my neck. He tugged me forward, his lips sealing our connection. His tongue swept across my lips, and I closed my mouth around it and sucked.

He groaned and his fingers clenched my ass, pulling me against him. Our stiff cocks ground against each other in a maddeningly good way. We'd both suffer for it later when we had to return to work with raging hard-ons. But I couldn't even find it in me to care in that moment. That's how good it felt to finally be touching him. Seemed like an eternity had passed since I last had the chance.

"What are you doing to me?' he grunted into my neck.

I looked over his shoulder, considering the room we were in. Bottles and cans were loaded on a large metal shelf near the wall.

"Over here," I said, nudging him behind the display. "Keep quiet."

"What the—" He cut off his own words with a groan as I pulled down his zipper and yanked his hard cock out.

When I got on my knees, his legs nearly buckled. My tongue swiped across the head, where a perfect bead of cum had escaped. "Fuck," he whispered.

"This is for having to watch me with other people," I said, before stuffing him in my mouth all the way down to the root.

"Ah, hell, that's—" he mumbled, grabbing onto my hair as my mouth bobbed up and down. His fingers tugged and it hurt like hell but turned me on to no end.

"I think about bending over for you," I said, licking his bulk lengthwise. "Even last night, I was so fucking hard because I imagined you getting naked with me."

I could taste more pre-come on my tongue. His eyes were closed and his mouth was hanging open in bliss. "Uuuhhh."

"Shit, I can't get you out of my head, and I hate the thought of not being with you again," I said, taking a long, slow lick around his crown and then up and down each side, around the base, and then back up to the head.

"I want you so fucking bad," he growled, his cock twitching like crazy in my hand.

"Show me how bad," I said. "Fuck my mouth."

Smoke grabbed my head more firmly and thrust his cock inside, the tip hitting the back of my throat. I relaxed my jaw to take him even further as my fingers reached behind him to squeeze his cheeks.

"The way you talk to me, hell. Even the sound of your voice lights me up like a forest fire every damn time," he said, his hips driving into my mouth. "I can't fucking get enough of you."

I could feel it. He was going to come. His legs were shaking, and as my fingertip swiped along the crease of his ass, the tang hit my mouth, and I gobbled down every damn drop.

I kept his cock between my lips, licking and sucking him dry until he begged me to stop. I pulled off, swiped my forearm across my chin, and looked up at him. "Mmmm, now I'll have the taste of you in my mouth all night."

He yanked me to my feet and shoved his tongue down my throat, tasting himself on me. The kiss felt so intimate that I never wanted it to end. It seemed to last forever as we clung to each other, both unwilling to let go.

When we heard voices in the club's office next door, Smoke jerked away, pulling his pants up in a flash, as if suddenly remembering the risk we had just taken.

"Hell, anybody could've walked in," he said, rushing his hands through his hair and returning to the box he was loading. "We can't keep doing shit like that."

"Fuck, I loved it, though," I said, pulling him back for one more kiss.

His fingers grazed over my zipper to my painful hard-on. "What about you?"

"All cool," I said, backing away. "I only wanted to taste you."

Smoke walked out the door with the box of beers he'd previously loaded, while I turned my back, hiding my own erection. I heard chatter from the Disciples' office and Cherry adjusting the rock music station on the stereo, and it was as if we had been in our own secret world behind that closed door. Still, we couldn't make a habit of that, not here in the middle of the day.

We worked until closing while the electricity crackled and coursed between us. And every time Smoke passed by me and stole a discreet glance at the front of my pants, my cock would jerk. "Asshole."

CHAPTER TWENTY
SMOKE

Over at Fish's clubhouse today, the same dude eyed me from the corner of the room. The difference this time was that he was sitting beside another guy who didn't even seem to notice. The other member had stared as well when I walked in the room, but his gaze was one of curiosity and maybe apprehension.

"What's his deal?" I asked Fish, who was standing beside his second in command.

"Sawyer?" he asked. "He's suspicious of you just like you are of him."

This was more than skepticism—the dude was totally checking me out. Was he trying to make me feel uncomfortable? Was that his angle? Nah, this was different. Almost like he wanted me to know he was into dudes. Had he guessed something about me? Fuck, all the more reason for me to remain neutral, not show him any of my cards.

When I looked over at them again, Sawyer had turned away. "What the hell is he suspicious about?"

"Somebody steering us the wrong way, getting us killed."

I nodded in understanding. "But you and Mal go way back, so we all should be cool, right?"

"No question," he said, tapping me on the shoulder. "But things have been known to happen. A little suspicion is always good, I say. Keeps everyone honest."

I liked that he was being open about this. It made me like him more and trust him a little better. Thing was, I was only a recruit and certainly not privy to his private conversations with Mal.

I didn't know the Scorpions' concrete plan, and maybe I wouldn't know until right before it happened. I hoped that Mal kept the Disciples totally out of this one. But sometimes other clubs needed backup. I would have been more than happy sitting this one out.

In the same back room as last visit, Fish pulled up a new video of the members of the Asylum.

My eyesight fuzzed as I took in the scene. It was footage of my old gang, laughing and smoking weed in some nondescript location. On one of the couches a couple of them were completely strung out, heads lolled back, as needles pricked skin.

I blinked repeatedly as I was hit with several overwhelming sensations at once. A chill stole across my shoulders, which in another second shifted to prickly heat as sweat dripped down the middle of my back. The same thing my Narcotics Anonymous sponsor said might happen to me over the years. That I might physically miss heroin. Like a carnal craving deep in my gut.

My throat worked to swallow while my stomach gurgled and then attempted to revolt as I gulped the warm bile back down. One scenario flicked repeatedly through my head like old film footage. Jake rubbing some coke—his drug of choice—on my lips, and then pulling me into a sex-hazed love fest behind closed doors.

I was thankful Jake wasn't on the screen in front of me; it might've officially sent me over the goddamn cliff.

I heard Fish's voice in the background, but I had no clue what he was saying. It was like suffering from heat stroke. As if the beating sun had zapped all of my energy and I could scarcely draw a breath, let alone focus on anything in front of me.

Fish roughly grabbed my arm. "You okay? If this is too much…"

"I'm good, just need some water," I said, coughing. "Feeling a little parched."

He snapped his fingers. "Bring him something to drink."

Water appeared in front of me, and I downed it in one shot. I took slow breaths in and out of my nose until finally everything jerked back into place. My fingers grasped the table in front of me. My feet were on the ground as I leaned forward in the chair.

"I'm cool," I said, avoiding the screen. "Repeat your question."

Fish stared at me for a long moment, concern apparent in his eyes, along with hesitation. Finally he looked back up at the video. "They get plastered like that a lot?"

"Once or twice a week." I chanced a brave glance at the screen again, which was frozen on a different location and slightly blurred. "Or at least, they used to."

"Jesus fuck," he said, probably staring at the spread of drug paraphernalia on the table in front of the Asylum.

They were packaging the white powder for storage or shipping. Terrence had rented warehouses to do the dirty work in several unassuming locations. "They're really into their product, if you know what I mean."

"Anyone on the lookout while they're all getting fucked up?"

I felt a pang in my chest. He wanted to know if that was the best time to do a raid. Except, a couple of years ago that could've been me. And I might've ended up dead because I'd been too plastered out of my mind even to help myself.

"I…" I shook my head. "I don't know."

"Hey, look, I'm not asking you to be responsible for what goes down," he grunted out. Probably had enough of my cowardly ass right about then. I needed to pull it the fuck together. "You're only here to give us some insight."

"I know that," I snapped. "It's just…I used to be one of those idiots sitting there getting high. That's all I cared about, man. I could've gotten my head blown off…if somebody hadn't saved my ass."

His voice softened. "Mal?"

I stared into his eyes, attempting to find some understanding there. I located it quickly. Either that or he was a good liar. But I didn't think so. Mal was a good judge of character, wasn't he?

"Fuck man, sorry," I said, sitting up and getting my wits about me. I didn't owe my old club anything. They had nearly ruined my life. "There were a couple of guys who didn't partake. Not many, though. But Terrence always used at least one lookout."

Fish lightly slapped my shoulder. "Thanks. That's all I needed to hear."

"Yeah, cool." I stood up and showed myself out the back door.

* * *

I rode out to the marina, to the place I always met Felix for patrol.

I saw Jude and Cory coming off the water with their wakeboards and fishing poles and smiled to myself at how content they looked. Nobody would fuck with them now. Still, I always kept an eye out.

But I envied their freedom as they held hands and walked toward Jude's place, where Cory had moved in shortly after their ordeal.

"Everything cool over at the Scorpions compound?" Felix asked after he motored closer to me. I tore my eyes away from the happy couple and nodded.

"I'll take the east end and meet you back here in an hour."

"Sounds good."

I sped away from the marina toward the freeway entrance and then back around, enjoying the feel of the wind on my back. I heard another motorcycle in the distance and wondered who it might be.

I didn't recognize the black insignia on his cut until he was practically on top of me from behind.

"What the hell you doing on our turf?" I asked a little too roughly as he pulled beside me. God, what the hell had I seen in him all those years ago? He looked tired and worn, like a guy who partied way too hard.

Jake smirked, the lines around his mouth drawing tight. "Not against the law."

I gripped my handlebars. "I know it was you who messed with our bartender. Mal is pissed. So am I. Vaughn's a good man."

He shrugged, but I saw the slight tremor in his eyes. Mal might've wanted to turn the club around, but he was still intimidating as hell. And he'd always protect his own, no matter what. "You've got no proof."

I ignored his denial and asked the bigger question instead. "Why him?"

"You fucking him?" he asked, his jaw ticking.

"What?" I scoffed in order to buy some time.

"You fucking the bartender?" He stared right into my eyes to search for the truth. I couldn't look away now or he'd spot my deceit.

"Course not," I said, gritting my teeth. "Only helping him out with the bar. He's short on staff and I know the business, remember?"

Something shifted in his gaze as he seemed to recollect how broken up I'd been about my dad dying in that fire. How vulnerable I'd seemed the first time he approached me about joining his club.

"Besides," I said, swiping my mouth against my arm. "He's not my type."

His eyes came alive at that lie. I was trying to throw him off the trail even though it was killing me even to talk to him. I wanted to jump off my bike and pound his skull into the asphalt for messing with the only person who'd made me feel things in a long-ass time.

"Maybe he's *your* type," I said. "Why else you got eyes on him?"

He shook his head. "Not him. *You.*"

So he was admitting to it. "What the fuck? It's been years. I—"

"I miss having you around. You and your tight ass," he said, his fingers making a fist on his lap. "Been nobody else like you."

I couldn't help the burst of anger that erupted like a popped blood vessel. "You mean you miss topping me, bossing me around, having somebody to poke with a needle?"

Somebody who'd become dependent on him. I nearly shuddered at the thought of the man I'd been reduced to because of that small white crystal heated on a spoon and pumped into my veins. I couldn't go down that road ever again.

I'd rather die first.

"Aw, man, you still got hard feelings about that?" His hand reached out, but I backed away from his touch.

"You helped jump-start my addiction, you bastard."

"You would've started it with or without me."

"Maybe so," I admitted. "But that's nothing to build a relationship on."

"Relationships are shit anyway," he said. Maybe he'd forgotten how he'd begged me never to leave his sorry ass. "No way for us to be out in the open, anyway."

I shook my head and tried to rid myself of the slimy feeling sneaking down my back just being in the same vicinity as him.

"I gotta go." I placed my feet on the pegs, my hands firm on the handlebars.

"Wait," he said, and I looked up at him. "So you're not into the bartender?"

"Fuck no," I said. "He likes pussy, anyway."

He shook his head as if confirming my suspicions that he'd been watching Vaughn.

"You like your share of pussy, too," he said. "But there's nothing like a good hard cock in your ass."

I inhaled a breath. "What the hell do you want from me?"

He lifted his shoulder in a shrug, like it was that simple. "Just a good fuck for old times' sake?"

I shivered at the idea of ever being naked with him again. Over my dead body.

I angled my head to the side. "Your club still doesn't know about you?"

He paled. "You know better than that. You wouldn't want your secret out, either."

"You better leave me the fuck alone or I'll have to take my chances. Mal would be more fair than Terrence, and you know it." My former leader was brutal and unapologetic. "Leave Vaughn alone. He's never done anything to you."

Before I could drive off, he got his fingers around my wrist. I yanked my arm away. "Why've you been out to the Scorpions clubhouse?" he demanded.

He definitely was keeping track of me. Fuck.

"You know he and Mal go way back," I said, rolling my eyes. "He's still got business dealings with him. What's it to you?"

He was grasping at straws; I could see it in his eyes.

"We hear you got bad blood with the Scorpions and a whole bunch of other clubs," I said, trying to rattle him. "The Asylum's gone downhill. Too much partying."

"Don't act like you don't remember how it used to all go down," he said, and I gritted my teeth.

"Is it true you're totally pulling out of guns?" he said. "You're going to be a sorry-ass broke club."

I could only imagine how rampant the rumors had been that we were a club in trouble. "What the hell do you care about how we run our business, anyway?"

"A bunch of pussies is what you've become."

I clenched my jaw. "You don't want to go up against us to find out."

He revved his engine.

"You leave the bartender alone," I said. "Mal's got eyes on him, anyway."

He cocked an eyebrow. "You come back to me, I won't bug him no more."

I spit the acidy taste in my mouth onto the pavement. "Fuck you."

I motored off in the opposite direction and then onto the freeway, completely out of sorts from this messed up day.

I'd make it though patrol and then find myself an NA meeting. Figure out my goddamn head.

CHAPTER TWENTY-ONE
VAUGHN

The following weekend, Smoke and I had stayed late closing up the Hog's Den. It wasn't something agreed upon. We simply lingered at the bar pretending to be busy until well after Lewis and Cherry left.

Smoke had been patrolling with Felix every night, which I'd admit brought me comfort. Outside of giving him head the other night, I hadn't been alone with him or had time to talk to him.

If the only way we could steal moments together was like this, under the premise of running the bar together, then so be it. It was better than nothing, though I couldn't even believe I was still entertaining any of those thoughts. What I really needed to do was move the hell on. But until he gave me a clue that he was doing the same, I wasn't sure I could.

He was stalling now just as much as I was as he placed the last of the chairs upside down on a table and I swept beneath before replacing the broom.

There'd been no club business in the back room tonight, so we were completely alone for the first time in days. My heart was battering in my chest at the thought of being closer to him. Smoke and I had cut out all the flirting in a silent agreement that it was too torturous from both ends.

But still I joked and yammered away with my regulars because I couldn't stop myself. Just how it was. Besides, it helped relieve the tension between Smoke's longing stares and lingering silences. We were like that Penn and Teller comedy routine. I'd set him up and he'd deliver the modest gesture or soft-spoken punch line at the exact right moment. He was quickly becoming a favorite behind the bar with certain customers, and not only the ladies.

"I ran into him a couple of nights ago on patrol." Smoke kept his voice low even though he knew there was nobody around.

I looked over his shoulder, just as a precaution. "Who?"

"Jake," he said, and my heart launched to my throat.

My fingers gripped the stool. "What—"

"I was right about my suspicions," he said, squeezing his eyes shut.

My elbows sank to the bar top. "He admitted it?"

"Not in so many words."

I balled the towel sitting near the tap. "He thought we were seeing each other?"

He nodded. "I set him straight. I hope it'll be cool."

"He still wants you," I said, and he neither agreed nor denied it. My stomach bunched into a tangled ball. Even though Jake was a sick fuck, I couldn't help feeling resentful.

"How did it feel seeing him after all this time?" I needed to ask. They had a history, after all.

"Filthy," he said, practically shivering. "Like I needed a shower. I wanted to knock his fucking teeth out for what he did to your place. But I needed to keep my cool."

"Smart," I said, and then straightened. "Guess we better still steer clear of each other in case…"

"Yeah," he said, looking as bummed as I felt about it.

I cut the last light and headed toward the exit like my boots were trudging through molasses.

An arm wound around me from behind before I was able to make it to the door.

Smoke's lips found my ear. "I want you so goddamn bad."

"So have me," I said, barely able to keep from trembling as his hot breath caressed my throat.

He growled and forced my shoulder against the wall as his hand snaked around front to palm my erection. I'd been aching for him for hours. Days. Maybe even years.

Neither of us spoke. The lights were out, and our heavy breaths echoed in the empty space. I could feel his heart jackhammering against my shoulder blades, and his dick was long and hard as granite against my ass.

His lips attacked my neck as his fingers unzipped my jeans.

He yanked my pants halfway down and shoved his finger along my crack.

Smoke groaned at the same time I did. "Fuck," I whispered.

"I've been hard for you all night," he said, digging a condom out of his pocket. "I've got no lube."

"We'll just have to—" Before I could get the words out, he flipped me around, my back making contact with the cold wall, and he sank to the floor in front of me.

Smoke was on his fucking knees in my empty bar, and the sight was enough to make me leak down the front of my pants. His mouth was like a warm oven and as his flushed lips encircled me, I gripped his head and gasped.

"I've been thinking about this cock," he said in that calm and determined manner. "How it tastes and smells, how this vein right here bulges when you're nearly there."

His tongue made slow licks up and down my length. I shuddered, my balls pulling up tight. The familiar sensation was already present at the base of my spine. When he deep-throated me, I nearly yelled out.

"It's so good." My hips began thrusting toward his mouth.

"You're going to come for me, and then I'm going to fuck you real good."

"Oh goddamn." His commanding, self-assured voice was getting to me. The one he seemed to reserve for me. I was right on the cusp. It had felt like too damn long.

He dragged his mouth away and watched me intently, reaching his fingers up to my lips. "Suck on them."

I pulled his middle and forefinger into my mouth and hollowed out my cheeks, mimicking the way he bobbed up and down my length, and nearly seeing stars.

He withdrew his fingers from my mouth as his lips kissed their way down to my balls. He licked and sucked while his hand snaked behind to run along my crease again.

He nudged both wet fingers inside. Uncomfortable at first, it soon turned to pleasure as he began pumping in time with my thrusts.

"I need to get inside you," he rasped, licking his way back up to my head. "I love your tight heat. Fuck, it's like no other."

And those words sent me bursting apart like an entire fucking galaxy of shooting stars, a supernova of orgasmic proportions. I spurted inside his mouth as everything around me blurred into a sweaty, hot, and heaving distortion.

Smoke pulled back after a couple swallows and watched in wonder as the rest of my come filled his palm and then ran down his arm and onto the floor.

I was a limp and mindless heap as his forearm firmly pinned my hips to the wall. He watched my eyes as I attempted to keep them trained on him. He licked at his wrist as if my come was a delicacy and then stood up to unbutton his pants.

"Put the condom on me." My fingers were numb, so I tore it open with my teeth. Before I rolled it over his length, I swiped my tongue across the bead of pre-come glistening there. "Ah shit, hurry."

With my come still dripping still from his fingers, he lubed his own cock. The very act was as dirty as it was erogenous.

I groaned and sank my head against the wall. He leaned forward and tenderly kissed my neck before sucking on a patch of skin at the hollow of my throat. I wanted him to leave his mark on me; I wanted to feel its burn the next day.

Smoke steered me to the nearest tabletop and urged my shoulders forward. My elbows sank and I dipped my head as I heard him rustle his jeans further down his hips.

"Fuck." I was a heaving, quivering mess, but when he pushed inside me using my own come as lube, I nearly sparked to life again.

Jesus Christ, if somebody could have seen me then, bent over the table in my own goddamn bar, giving it up to Smoke as his teeth nibbled at my shoulder and he mumbled unintelligibly. I fucking loved it. Loved hearing him come undone over me.

His arm wrapped around my chest and he held me almost possessively as he thrust harder. My sweaty T-shirt stuck against his chest. He licked along my hairline and then gripped my chin to claim my mouth.

"I don't know if I'd had better than you," he said in a pained voice. "And it's completely fucking with my head."

"Tell me about it," I said as I angled my jaw to meet his lips in a sloppy and desperate kiss.

He kept his arm slung around me in an intimate hold as his pounding became erratic and I knew he was about to break apart. He shouted my name as he came, and there was no sweeter sound I'd ever heard.

* * *

The following morning, I showered, changed, and called my dad on the way to the store. Usually I got what I thought he needed, but sometimes he threw in extra requests. He didn't answer, though, so maybe he was in the shower.

I had mounted one of those handgrips in his bathroom, and though he grumbled the entire way through installation, I knew he was grateful that he wasn't going to slip and fall in the water collecting at the bottom of the tub. That surgery had taken a toll on him, and even if he never admitted it, he needed all the help he could get.

I tried him one more time in the parking lot, and he still didn't pick up. I pushed aside the gnawing feeling in my chest that something was wrong. He'd done this to me on other occasions, when he'd been napping nowhere near his phone.

He'd been way more tired than usual lately, so maybe he had fallen asleep in his chair.

Still, I picked up the pace in every aisle and loaded only the necessities before heading for the checkout.

I kept the speed limit to my dad's place but left the groceries in the car so I could check on him first thing.

When I called out for him and he still didn't respond, my chest tightened painfully. I didn't find him in front of the television or in his bedroom.

"Pop?" I called.

A grunting noise echoed down the hallway. Fuck, I was right, he had fallen down.

When I entered the bathroom, he lay half dressed on the floor, his pants unbuttoned, his shirt hanging partway off his shoulder as if he were about to turn on the tap.

"What the hell happened?" I reached for my phone after I bent down to prop his head on my knee.

He didn't speak, only stared with glazed eyes, so I tapped out the emergency number.

"Hang on, Dad," I said, stroking his arm. "The ambulance is on the way."

CHAPTER TWENTY-TWO
SMOKE

I stepped into an empty bar, surprised that I'd beat Vaughn there. My gaze couldn't help wandering to the table I had taken him on the previous night. Damn, he was amazing and thoroughly wrecking my brain.

Anybody could've walked in and I wouldn't have given two shits. I wanted him that badly. And the fact that he'd given it up to me, allowed me to fuck him in his own establishment, had said a lot. Showed that he'd needed me just as much.

Except now I sought him out every single day. A look, a kiss, a touch. I simply needed him in some capacity, which was really disorienting and fucking complicated. And I didn't know how to fix it. Because it was as if he were already in my blood, saturating my veins. In some ways mimicking what that other addiction had become.

As I got situated behind the bar, the door opened, and I held my breath. But it was only Cherry. I liked the girl, and her old man was pretty cool as well. It felt like she had Vaughn's back and would never betray the club.

"Vaughn's not here yet?" she asked, looking around, as shocked as I had been.

"Nope," I said, restocking the vodka. "Must be running late."

"Maybe he had something to do for his old man."

I nodded as she made her way to the back room to put her things away.

My cell buzzed right then. It was Vaughn. We'd exchanged phone numbers when I started working at the bar, but we had yet to call one another. So I was surprised to see his name pop up.

"I need your help," he said as soon as I answered.

"Anything," I said without hesitation.

His voice sounded strained. "My dad suffered a heart attack. He's in the hospital."

"Fuck, I'm sorry," I said, rustling my fingers through my hair. "What can I do?"

He paused, and I heard what sounded like beeping, which probably meant he was standing in the hospital hallway.

"Probably going to be here for a few more hours while they run tests," he said hesitantly. "He was practically unconscious when I found him, but he's come around since then. Still, they need to determine the extent of t he damage."

"Shit," I said, imagining him wandering alone in the hospital. "I'd offer to keep you company, but I'm going to assume the best thing for me to do is to keep the bar afloat tonight?"

"That would really help," he said in a rush, as if I'd pull the offer. "Thank you, Reed."

My heart thrummed in my chest. He'd called me Reed. It might've been a slip, and I wouldn't call him on it. But I liked him using it.

"I've got it covered on my end," I said. "Cherry, Lewis, and I will be fine tonight."

"Appreciate it," he said, blowing out a breath. "You get stuck on anything, call me."

"You just be there for your dad," I said, now pacing the entirety of the bar, my mind already creating a checklist of what was left to do before the customers came calling.

"Will do," he said. "Ring me at closing time? I'd appreciate that."

"You got it," I said. "And Vaughn? No worrying about us. I mean it."

After I filled Cherry in on what was happening, we got to work opening the bar.

Thankfully the night flew by, and it wasn't nearly as crowded as it could've been.

When Mal strode through the back door, he looked down the length of the bar for Vaughn, his gaze landing back on me. It did feel strange here without the head honcho. Vaughn was the heart and soul of this place and without him, it would never be the same.

"His dad had a heart attack," I said quietly when I got to Mal's end, out of the earshot of curious customers. Up until that point, I had been telling anybody who'd asked—which was pretty much everybody—only that he was taking the night off. Cherry had added that he deserved it, following my lead. "We've got it covered while he stays with him at the hospital."

"Shit," he said, tapping his fingers on the bar. "We could've closed the joint for the night."

"What, you think I can't handle this place on my own?" I cocked an eyebrow at him.

He laughed. "You actually look good behind that bar."

"I almost inherited a place like this a few years back, remember?" I said, resting my elbows on the bar.

He nodded, his eyes softening. "You miss it?"

I looked down the line of customers. Somehow their quiet chatter was soothing. Always had been. My dad would say it meant folks were content. "Dunno. I certainly feel comfortable here, and I'm glad to help out."

"I'm glad, too," he said, thumping me on the shoulder. "Vaughn has had a shit ton of luck this last month, yeah?"

I couldn't help thinking his trouble had begun directly after getting involved with me. Damn, he didn't need any more headaches. I'd do all I could to help out.

"Well, whatever he needs," Mal said, bringing me out of my thoughts. "We'll be happy to do it."

"I'll be sure to let him know."

"Hey," one of the regulars, Lou, yelled from the other end of the bar. "You gonna spend the rest of the night gossiping or you going to serve me a beer?"

"Better shut that trap or you'll be out on your ass," Mal said around a smile.

"You'd need five of yeh to take me," he said, and the whole bar erupted into laughter, including Lou, because he was an older gentleman, maybe in his seventies. He was here most nights and probably considered these guys family.

I served dozens more drinks over the course of the next few hours as Cherry racked up tips at the tables by serving pitchers and wings.

I certainly didn't have Vaughn's charisma or his flair for storytelling, but I think I held my own. It felt like good, honest work and I was glad to be able to hold down the fort for him. It also made me a bit proud of myself that I could do it on my own—outside of Lewis and Cherry's help of course.

Around closing time, the same woman who had gone home with Vaughn the other night slipped through the door, wearing high heels and an expensive silk blouse. Her gaze searched around for Vaughn, and I couldn't help the well of jealousy that arose in my gut. It was ridiculous, for sure, but she seemed to be back for a second round.

"Can't believe Vaughn gave that woman the time of day the other night," Cherry said low in my ear.

"Why is that?" I asked, now more curious than ever.

"She likes to kiss and blab," she said. "And Vaughn doesn't usually hook up with customers. Not sure what his deal was that night."

I cleared my throat and looked away as she continued. "She was in here the next day telling a group of ladies what a gentleman he'd been."

I sprang back in surprise. "A gentleman, huh?"

"Yeah. Guess he didn't close the deal that time, if you know what I mean," she said, and I felt my chest tighten. "So she must be back here to get her some."

Vaughn hadn't slept with her that night?

I shrugged. "Nothing wrong with wanting some meaningless sex when the mood strikes."

"I'm not against her hoping to hook up with Vaughn. It's her snitching about it everywhere that gets me," she said. "Anyway, I've been working with

Vaughn a long time. I'll bet he only left with her to get his mind off something else that night. Or some*one* else."

A line of heat climbed its way up my neck. Did Cherry know something was up? Or was she only trying to pick my brain?

My mouth became dry, and I had a hard time forming any kind of response. But by this time, Cherry was used to my silence. She knew I wasn't a big talker. Unless I was behind closed doors with Vaughn. Then I couldn't help myself. The man made me that crazy with need.

"I think he was hurt real good by somebody way back when," she said. "He deserves better."

Little did she know the somebody she was referring to had been a man. Or maybe she did, considering the way she was now staring me down.

Before I could reply, the woman in question interrupted us.

I walked away to finish last call while Cherry explained that Vaughn wasn't around tonight.

After all was said and done and I was the last man standing, I pulled out my phone and dialed Vaughn.

"How's your dad doing?" I asked.

"Better," he said, sounding more relaxed. "Though he's not the best patient."

I laughed, remembering how ornery my own father could be.

"They've got him settled in a room, but they're awaiting one more test before they take him back for a procedure."

"They're going to do the procedure tonight?"

"Or early morning. Guess the first twenty-four hours after a heart attack are the most crucial."

"Makes sense. Can I do anything else for you?"

He paused. "I know you've already done enough, but—"

"Just name it."

"Can you check on my cats?" he asked. "They should be fine, but soon enough they'll need to eat."

"I'm on it," I said, heading to his desk drawer where he explained his spare key was located. "Got it. I'll feed them in the morning, too, unless I hear from you first."

"No, you don't have to—"

"Consider it done," I said, hopping on my bike and then tucking my phone away.

I headed over to Vaughn's, parked in the lot, and let myself inside.

I called to his cats, but they didn't appear, which didn't surprise me. I found the food, and they sprinted toward their bowls when they heard me open the can. Humans and animals weren't that dissimilar when it came to basic needs.

One of the felines—Cane I think—was larger than the other, and he rubbed against my legs before attacking his bowl of chow.

I sat on the couch and watched them for a few minutes, and before I knew it, I had dosed off.

I was so damn exhausted, I could've curled up right there, and I considered it in my sleepy haze. But I knew that was a bad idea, especially if Vaughn made it home, so I forced myself to get up and leave.

After crawling between my own sheets, I texted Vaughn.

Me: All is well with your feline friends.

Vaughn: Great. Dad's surgery scheduled in a couple hours. Going to nap on the pull-out couch in his room. Catch you later.

I fell asleep promptly with my phone in my hand.

CHAPTER TWENTY-THREE
SMOKE

The following morning, I showered, slugged back coffee, and then texted Vaughn.

Me: How did the surgery go?

Vaughn: As well as can be expected. He's in recovery.

Me: Good news.

Vaughn: I'm heading to my dad's place to pick up a couple of things and then back to the hospital. I should be able to open tonight.

Me: Don't even think about it. Cherry and I got it covered.

Vaughn: We'll see. Thanks for everything.

Me: Don't thank me yet. I'm out the door to feed your cats again. They might fall in love with me and not care if you come home again.

Vaughn: You bastard. I can totally see Cane falling for you. But no need to do that. I'm going to stop home later this morning.

Me: Already done.

I didn't know what it was that compelled me to check on his place again. I just wanted to do something nice for Vaughn, I guess.

But as soon as I opened that apartment door, I knew something was way off. There was a soft keening sound coming from the bedroom, and my limbs locked up. I was afraid of what I'd find. Fuck, had I fed his cats the wrong food or something?

I searched around the living room and kitchen, but nothing else seemed out of sorts. Was the cat sick?

Near the foot of Vaughn's bed, the black cat lay on its side on the carpet. A faint aroma of something sweet hung in the room.

Cane was sniffing and circling, but the smaller cat was so sick, she looked practically comatose. I could see her chest moving up and down from labored breaths.

"Hey buddy," I said, gently lifting her up. The sharp trace of alcohol assaulted my nostrils. When I leaned closer, I could smell the whiskey on her whiskers. What the fuck?

Did she get into some liquor? That's when I spotted a bottle of peach schnapps lying near the closet door. Where in the hell had that come from?

The cat shuddered out a breath and then went limp in my arms. Her little chest was still pumping air but shit, this animal needed help. I held her closer while I dug out my phone and dialed Felix.

"Pick me up at Vaughn's place in the Chevelle?" I said. "Need help pronto. I'll explain later."

I reached down and stroked the other cat's head, and he mewled in response. Then I lifted the bottle of schnapps from the floor. Looked like only the one cat had gotten into it.

I headed to the kitchen and pulled open Vaughn's cupboards. The other bottles of booze were stored on a high shelf above the stove, and that's when it became alarmingly evident that this was no accident. This had been foul play.

I found a carrier in Vaughn's front closet and gently laid the cat inside. The other cat circled the cage, so I made a split-second decision to bring him along as well.

Felix arrived within minutes.

"You grew up with cats," I said, placing the carrier in the back seat. "Is alcohol lethal to them?"

"They get into some?" he asked while pulling out of the drive. "Just a small amount could cause death."

"Fuck," I said, looking back at those defenseless animals one last time. "I need to get that cat to the vet."

"Is that why it reeks in here?"

"Shit." I smacked my hand on the dash, furious with the one person I figured must've spotted me leaving Vaughn's place late last night.

A flash of a long-ago memory came to me of Jake, eyes dilated from snorting coke, attempting to light a stray cat's tail on fire. Sick motherfucker.

Now I just wanted revenge.

Felix didn't ask any more questions as we pulled into the vet's parking lot. When they saw the condition of the cat, they took her back immediately, along with the second feline, as a precaution.

After waiting for what seemed like forever, the doctor finally emerged from the exam room.

"We had to pump her stomach. She should pull out fine," she said, smiling. "Though I would caution you to never leave open alcohol containers on the counter."

Instead of responding, I just nodded, allowing her to formulate her own thoughts.

"We'll have to keep the cat for observation. You can take the other little guy home. He has a clean bill of health."

Felix drove me to get my bike, and then I met him at home with the other cat.

"What the fuck is going on here, Smoke?" he asked when I leaned over the back seat to grab the carrier.

"Somebody's screwing with Vaughn," I said. "I need to talk to Mal about it first."

"Same guy who broke into his place a couple weeks back?"

"Pretty sure."

"Was it somebody he fucked over?" he said, pushing the automatic garage door closed. "That doesn't seem like Vaughn."

"I promise to fill you in after I talk to Mal," I said, and he nodded.

"I won't say a word to the guys," he said. "Let me know if you need anything else."

After taking the gray cat up to my place, where he promptly sprinted and hid beneath the couch, I made the long trek to the compound, which was about a twenty-five-minute drive from the city. The ride down on the back country roads had always been a pleasant drive, but today it felt drawn out as the scenery blurred and melded right along with my thoughts.

My skin felt tight to the bursting point, like I couldn't hold everything in any longer, no matter the outcome. It was time to tell the prez what was going down.

The main room was empty save for a couple of recruits. I knew Mal was in the office because I had called beforehand to be certain he was there. Asked him to stay put because it was important.

I closed the door and slumped in the chair across from his desk.

He leaned back, taking in my appearance. For all I knew, worry lines were etched across my forehead. I could almost feel the grooves. "You look like hell. What's up?"

"I…shit," I said, inhaling a steady breath. This was going to be tougher than I thought. "I offered to help Vaughn out while he stayed at the hospital with his dad, so I went to his place to feed his cats."

Mal stared hard at me, and then his gaze drifted down to my fingers, which were gripping the armrest. "And?"

"Somebody had been in there again," I said. "Messed with his cat."

His face turned dark. "Messed how?"

"Fed it alcohol," I bit out and clenched the chair. "Cat went into a coma."

"Fuck," he growled. "You sure?"

I nodded. "No way to mistake the smell on that cat's whiskers. Plus there was an empty bottle lying on the ground. Wanted us to find it."

"Vaughn give you any idea who might be—"

"I know who's fucking with Vaughn," I said, cutting him off at the pass. "And it has to do with me."

He sat up straight and narrowed his eyes. "What about you?"

I breathed in deeply. "Somebody from my old club."

"What the fuck you talking about?" he demanded, his voice laced with worry. "You mean they got wind of you helping Fish?"

Before I could even respond, he was working it out in his own head. "Nah, that don't make no sense. If they found out, why would they be messing with Vaughn? Speak up, boy."

"It's somebody I…" I choked out the words. "It's Jake."

"Jake the Snake?" He leaned forward, and I could feel sweat trickling down my neck. "What about him?"

Goddamn, this was hard.

"We…hung out a lot," I said, looking at floor. "He was the guy who introduced me to my first shot of heroin."

"Shit," he said, shaking his head as if remembering those days. "And?"

"He was…or maybe still is…kind of fixated on me."

"What the living hell do you mean *fixated*?" he rumbled. "Out with it."

"We…him and I…Mal, I'm…" I muttered. "I'm bisexual."

"The fuck?" Mal sprang up on that revelation and began pacing with a crazed look in his eyes.

It was already out. No way to take it back, so I simply kept on going. "And he might think that since I've been hanging around Vaughn lately, that…that he's my boyfriend."

Mal's face turned tomato-red as if he couldn't even believe what he was hearing. He didn't breathe a word, his jaw ticking away, his mind probably going a mile a minute.

"I…listen, I've always kept that part of myself private," I said. "I would never do anything to jeopardize—"

"Did they know about the two of you?" He spun on me and stalked over to my chair. I clenched my fists on my knees, thinking maybe he was going to slug me. "The Asylum club?"

"No way," I said, and his features relaxed a bit. "Seems he's been keeping track of me all on his own, hoping we could finish where we left off."

"What in the living hell did you ever see in that douchebag?" he asked, as if to himself. I had asked myself a similar question plenty of times.

"By the time I figured out what a fuck-up he really was, I was already an addict. Only cared about the next hit, if I'm keeping it real. He kept me supplied." Mal stared up at the ceiling, trying to wrap his head around what I was saying. "I was young and desperate and dumb. Learned plenty since then. I could never be with that bastard again."

Mal's gaze swung back to me, and he studied me for what seemed like days. "You're attracted to both men and women?"

"Been with women, mostly," I mumbled. "Haven't been with too many men."

He folded his arms. "But you were with Jake?"

"Got high with him mostly, but yeah." I wouldn't confess how he demanded sex all the time and was nearly insatiable. Just the memory of being with him made me want to dry heave right there on the floor.

Mal visibly swallowed, and there was a small tremor in his fingers.

"And now Vaughn is being dragged into this because you're helping him out with his bar?"

I simply nodded, not wanting the wrong words to betray me.

"Don't make no sense," he said. "You're with our boys all the time. What am I missing here?"

Hell, I had no intention of outing Vaughn. I had no place doing that. One shocker for the day was enough.

"Maybe because we close up late together and I've…been out to his place a couple of times," I said, trying to make it sound plausible. "I'm considering making him a piece for his fireplace. We've become friends. He's a good guy."

Fuck, I might've been digging myself deeper. But I preferred the boom to come down on me. Vaughn could stay out of it.

"And he isn't technically one of us," Mal said, tapping his fingers on the desk. "So suddenly Jake's curious because you've never hung out with Vaughn before?"

"Probably. The asshole had tunnel vision when it came to sex," I said, wincing. Mal didn't meet my eyes, but I followed through with my thought anyway. "Always thinking with the wrong head."

"Shit. Fuck," he said, and then he took an awfully long time thinking things through while I flexed my feet on the hard floor, attempting to find purchase. "I don't want to mess with the Scorpions operation, but when it all comes down, I will nail that asshole to the wall."

I caught his eye. "I want to myself, believe me."

"You think this is all it is?" he asked. "He doesn't know about you working with Fish?"

I could've told him about my run-in with Jake the other night, but Mal trusted us to give him the straight facts no matter how we came to them. "Don't think so."

"And you're sure it's him—who's messing with Vaughn?"

"I don't have proof, but I know it in my gut," I said, picturing what happened the night of the break-in. "The way he left Vaughn's place, some of the things in his bedroom—"

He held up his hand. "I don't even want to know."

We sat silently for a bit and I chewed on the side of my gum, trying to muster the courage to voice what I needed to say. And maybe he was waiting for it, too.

"I'm sorry," I said, forcing the words out. "If you want me to—"

"What the fuck you talking about?" he roared. "I would be some backward-ass leader if I allowed something like this to bring our club down. You're a good man. Like a little brother to me."

Hell, he called me a brother. Not just a Disciples brother, a flesh-and-blood brother. I felt like I was still deceiving him by not coming clean about Vaughn and me. But that was something I needed to discuss with the man himself. No way was I going to share any of his secrets.

"We all got our kinks," Mal said, swinging his hand as if to sweep it all away. "That's why most people keep them private."

I wanted to tell him that being gay or bisexual was not a kink, but I was already skating on thin ice.

"I feel terrible that I caused trouble for Vaughn," I said. "Maybe you should take me off patrol. Find somebody else for the bar."

'No." He shook his head fervently. "I want to do just the opposite."

I nearly choked on my own saliva. "What the hell do you mean?"

He leaned over the desk. "He trusts you, yeah?"

I narrowed my eyes. "I…I don't know."

"Yeah, he does. It's settled then," he said, sitting back in his chair. "Vaughn stays out at your place with Felix so that you guys are always with him."

"What the fuck kind of idea is that?" I nearly leapt out of my chair. "Why not send him to live with his dad?"

"So something could happen to his old man?" he asked. "I'm not going to have that on my conscience."

"I wasn't thinking. Fuck," I said, shaking my head. "How about he takes a temporary room out here?"

"Going to guess it'd be too far from the bar and his old man."

I opened my mouth to refute that, but nothing came out.

"Why you fighting this?" he asked, narrowing his eyes. "You worried if Vaughn finds out about you, he's gonna want to bolt—"

"No, nothing like that." Christ. If only he knew how backward he had it. And when he found out, we might both be out on our asses.

"We put eyes on your place at night. Felix is there for added protection," he said, steely determination in his face. "We keep this our club's business for now."

"Aren't the brothers going to ask the same questions?"

"Keep your preferences under wraps. Tell them later if you want."

"Shit," I said. "Some of those guys are going to think I've been giving them the eye this whole time."

Mal stared at me. "But that's not how it works, right?"

"Fuck no. You want to screw every damn female that steps in your path?"

He steepled his fingers in front of him. "I see your point."

"Who the fuck wants to hook up with those assholes anyway?" I asked around a smirk. "Half those greasy motherfuckers can't even wash their pits properly."

That got a bark of laughter out of Mal.

"Look, nobody comes on our turf and messes with our family," he said and then pounded his fist on the desk. "That scumbag tries something again, we take him out."

Fuck, what was Mal thinking with this plan?

"Isn't that only asking for trouble?"

"It's calling him out of his hidey hole," he said. "His club is going down, anyway. It's only a matter of time."

The craziest thing of all was that Mal didn't even think to ask the one big question. The most obvious one. But I supposed his brain wasn't wired to think that way. He would never suspect that Vaughn was bisexual as well, because he probably never imagined that the world was so many different shades of queer. Not the world he lived in.

CHAPTER TWENTY-FOUR
VAUGHN

Me: Where the hell are my cats?

Smoke: Fuck, was hoping to tell you before you went home. Gonna give you a call right now. Some shit has hit the fan.

I was bringing my father home from the hospital in a couple of days and already had home health care lined up. He had rejected temporary assisted living and was refusing to let me stay with him, so a daily visit from a nurse was the next best option. Stubborn old coot.

He would recover fine, according to the doctors, but with his hip problems, mobility would become a struggle. I certainly hadn't seen any of this coming, but I knew he was getting up there in age and would eventually need more help.

I made it to the bar that afternoon, and in my quick scan around the joint, I could see that everything was still in order. Smoke and Cherry had done a nice job of keeping things going for me, but truth be told, I was glad to get back to work.

The bar was my life, and I needed to feel grounded again after practically living at the hospital the past twenty-four hours. But things had spun out of control, even in my absence. I mean, Christ, my cats were staying with Smoke, and I couldn't keep relying on him to help me out with every little thing.

I'll admit I was freaked and more than a little pissed that this motherfucker continued to mess with me.

Smoke had said that he told Mal about his relationship with Jake and that Mal had taken it as well as could be expected. But he had stopped short of divulging anything about us, said it was my business to tell. I considered saying fuck it, because everything else was turned upside down anyway, but for now, I'd follow Smoke's lead.

I knew Mal wanted to talk to me himself about the plan going forward, so when I heard movement from the back room, I expected the prez to be waiting for me. "Vaughn, come on back and see me."

I steadied my breaths and headed toward his office.

"What's up, Mal?" I said, trying to act like nothing at all had changed, when I knew damn well everything had.

He got right down to business. "You've had a crap month with your dad in the hospital and your place being broken into."

I nodded because it was true. On the flip side, I'd also had one of the greatest months of my life. Outside of amazing sex, I'd found another man I connected with on a level I didn't even know existed before. Even though we couldn't have each other, the experience had opened up something inside me that had been locked away tight.

"Smoke brought you in the loop, yeah?" he said almost tentatively. "About him and Jake."

I crossed my ankle over my knee. "Right."

"You and him still cool?" He was asking whether Smoke telling me he was bisexual had bothered me. Couldn't be further from the truth.

"Of course," I said, waving him off. "No big deal."

"You're a good man, Vaughn. Like family to us. You don't need no more shit happening." His eyes softened as I watched him. "I'm sorry you were brought into Smoke's business, and because of it, I want you protected 24-7."

"I appreciate that," I said. I figured the only thing to do was never to have Smoke at my place again. But fuck, I hadn't even had time to check on my cats or anything. I'd pick them up from him and be done. "But—"

"No buts about it," he rumbled. "I want you to stay with Smoke, if you're cool with that. If Smoke isn't around, Felix will be in on my game plan, too.

You might not know him as well, but he's good for it. And my boys will be keeping their eye on you right where they can find you."

My mouth hung open in shock as my heart pummeled in my chest. No wonder Smoke didn't want to tell me this convoluted plan himself.

"And you think me staying with Smoke ain't going to raise a red flag?" A rainbow flag was more like it.

"Nobody's going to try to intimidate us, thinking we've gone soft or something, you feel me? That fucker is going down," he said. "Jake tries to mess with you again, he's going to have to do it on our turf."

"And if I refuse your plan?" I asked a little too quickly.

He pushed back from the desk, his eyes wide. It was his turn to look stunned.

"I get it, man, if you're not cool staying with somebody who prefers both— you know. I'm still trying to wrap my head around it." He stood up and paced.

Well, fuck, now I was creating more suspicion and trouble.

"I know Felix uses his spare room for weight training, but maybe he or one of the other guys could—"

"Nah, forget I said anything," I said. "It's just hard not being in my own space, you know?"

"I hear you." He studied me a long moment, and I nearly wilted under the scrutiny. "But think of it as doing me a favor. Jake comes anywhere near their place, he's gone."

"I suppose it's a good plan," I said, adjusting myself in my seat. "Smoke's a good guy. He saved my cats. Been a big help here at the bar. I feel bad putting him out."

"You got a problem with my lumpy couch?" I practically jumped out of my skin when I heard Smoke's voice from the doorway. I needed to recover quickly.

"I'd rather sleep on a blow-up mattress than that fire hazard," I said, grinning.

"Done," he said, shoving his hands in his pockets. I turned away quickly before I was caught staring. "Besides, I think those cats of yours already laid claim to my couch."

Mal burst out laughing. "I can't even picture you with pets."

"Right? If there's anybody who's going to suffer from this plan, it's him," I said, joining in on the ribbing. Smoke folded his arms and chomped good-naturedly on his gum. "We should've started him out small, broke him in a with a fish."

"Fuck you," Smoke said, laughing. "I'll clear the boxes in my guest bedroom and set you up in there. At least I know how to make a decent pot of coffee."

Mal seemed to be watching our exchange with interest. It was growing too domestic and cozy for my taste. I was nervous he'd read more into it, so I stood up.

"Gotta get to work," I said. "Smoke, I'll figure out the logistics with you after I check in with my pop and grab some things from my place."

A few minutes after I left Mal's office, Smoke appeared on the other side of the bar. "You sure you won't need an extra set of hands here tonight?"

"You've done plenty for me already," I said. "And you're about to do plenty more. Giving up your space like that for me."

Smoke looked over his shoulder, wondering if Mal could still hear us. "It'll all be cool, and it'll be nice to hang out…or whatever…"

His words faded out as his eyes fastened on mine, the raw emotions plainly evident on his face.

Every molecule occupying the space between us began to crackle and pulse.

Me staying with Smoke? Fuck.

As if he could read my thoughts, he backed away. "Catch you later."

CHAPTER TWENTY-FIVE
SMOKE

The first night Vaughn stayed with me, we played it cool, both of us on edge that anybody would think we were messing around. Even behind closed doors. We'd been stupid enough the other night with Felix right below us, too on fire for each other to care.

So he stayed in the guest bedroom that I finally made livable, and I restrained myself from charging in there in the middle of the night and pulling him into my bed.

It was like we were living in a concrete prison of our own suffocating sexual tension. On the other hand, the idea of having somebody to come home to every night actually felt nice. It was a thought that had never crossed my mind before.

The following morning, I made coffee, Vaughn scrambled some eggs, and we ate breakfast in silence. As if we couldn't truly enjoy each other's company. I knew it was harder on him than it was on me, so I made as many concessions with the space as I could, leaving him his own key to my place.

For the next couple of days we saw each other only in passing as he got his dad situated at home and then left to manage the bar. I was putting in hours at the auto parts shop, in addition to working on a new piece that had come as a surprise even to me.

The Scorpions would be dealing with the Asylum soon, calling them out on their sins, and who knew what might happen after that. One of the reasons Mal pulled back on all of our gun dealings was that he didn't like the idea of being controlled by the mafia. His dad might've seen it as a lucrative trade, but not when you were practically selling your own soul.

With any luck my problem with Jake would go away and things would return to normal for Vaughn. As normal as they possibly could be.

It felt freeing in a way to have confessed my business to Mal, even though it was only a partial truth. I'd catch Mal staring from time to time, as if he were trying to figure it all out—figure *me* out. He was decent about it, more decent than I'd given him credit for. Maybe I had Cory and Jude to thank for that.

When Vaughn texted me that he was leaving the bar, I said my goodbyes to Felix, who would call up another recruit to patrol the rest of the night.

"This situation got your internal clock all messed up?" Felix asked.

I sighed. "Isn't it always?"

He shrugged. "I've gotten used to sleeping during the day."

"It was becoming that way for me too," I said. "Until…you know, the current mess."

Felix and I were close to receiving our official patches, which was why we were training new recruits to run patrol. If I got glowing reviews from Fish, I'd be well on my way to earning my chops for the club. If Felix caught up with Jake, he'd get his stripes for sure.

"Wait," Felix said and then cleared his throat. "What is this beef really about with Jake the Snake?"

I should've known Felix would ask questions. He definitely deserved some answers. He'd been patient with me long enough.

Still, I chose my words carefully. "Jake introduced me to heroin. We got high together all the time."

"Asshole." His eyes softened at the news. He knew what an uphill battle I'd had to beat the drug. "Why is he trying to mess with Vaughn?"

What did I say now? We were in charge of keeping each other safe. Felix was the closest brother I had.

"Afraid if I tell you, you'll think differently of me," I said, wincing. "I'm ashamed of a lot of things. This isn't one of them, but you might see it otherwise."

"Hey, man, we've all got a history," he said. "I did some fucked up shit as well."

"If I tell you…" I said, still working up the nerve. "Promise to keep it to yourself until this is all over?"

"I swear it," he said, holding out his fist for a bump. "You're my brother."

I met his fist and then held his gaze, trying to read behind his eyes. He was a good guy through and through. Out of all the recruits, I'd expect him always to have my back.

"Jake and me, we…messed around a bit," I said as uneasiness gripped my stomach. "He had a thing for me, probably more than I did for him."

Felix's momentary look of shock passed quickly. "So you saying you're queer?"

"I'm bisexual," I said. "I like both men and women. Though I've mostly been with women."

"Hey, I'm cool with that," he said almost immediately. "My brother's gay."

"The brother who's in college?" Suddenly my chest felt lighter. He talked to his brother regularly on the phone, so they must've had a decent relationship. "Huh, go figure."

At least Felix had the courtesy not to say anything cliché like I didn't look the part or some shit like that.

"So how did Vaughn get dragged into this? Is Jake sweet on him?" he asked. "He is a good-looking dude. Even I can admit to that."

I laughed. He definitely was gorgeous. "I think since I've been helping him with the bar and stuff…"

"Ah, got it, no need to elaborate," he said, effectively letting me off the hook. "Dude is jealous, still got a thing for you."

He saved me from having to explain it on my own. He didn't suspect anything was going on between Vaughn and me after all.

When all this was said and done, Vaughn and I would have some decisions to make going forward. The easiest route would be for us to part ways and consider us history.

But who was that easy for? Me, or everybody else? Just the idea of never tasting and smelling Vaughn again caused my chest to squeeze so tight it was as if I was wearing a straightjacket.

"I'd better get going," I said, more than anxious to be with the man we'd been discussing. "Vaughn is being a good sport about all of this. Don't want to get on his bad side."

"We're going to owe him big time," Felix said, tossing me a final wave.

"No kidding," I mumbled, heading off in the other direction.

I turned on the stereo to Vaughn's favorite classic rock station and was waiting for him when he finally got inside. As soon as the door shut, I advanced on him. "I need you in my bed."

"Thank fuck," he said, and then sealed his mouth over mine for a deep and slow and all-consuming kiss. It was so hot I felt electricity buzzing through all of my limbs. I stumbled back in a daze when he released me, and I could tell that he thrived on making me weak in the knees.

"Shit," I said. "You drive me fucking wild."

"That makes two of us."

He backed me toward my bedroom like he was a predator and I was definitely his prey, pulling my shirt over my head while we both kicked out of our shoes and pants. He had his T-shirt yanked over his neck before hitting the bed. I would let him have the upper hand for now, but I was just itching to flip him over and fuck the hell out of him. He was nuzzling my neck and sucking on my collarbone, marking me where nobody else would see. I was squirming beneath him, my fingers grazing over every part of his body that I could reach. After I slid his boxers down, I fisted his cock in my hand while he straddled my hips. He bucked against me and groaned.

"I missed this," I said, shamelessly. "The way you smell and the sound of your voice, all raw and needy."

"Christ, you're going to make me blow my load too early," he grunted out.

He prodded my shoulder, encouraging me to flip onto my stomach. I resisted.

"Turn over for me."

"Why?" I said, hesitating. "What do you have in mind?'

"Christ, just do it. I'm not going to try to fuck you," he said, and my muscles unwound. "I should be allowed to touch you when I want."

After I twisted onto my stomach, my stiff cock digging into the sheets, his lips found that one spot beneath my ear that drove me insane. He bit and licked lightly, and for the first time I wondered if he missed topping. Would he seek out other guys to get his needs met? A flaming coal of possessiveness blazed in my stomach, burning me up from the inside.

His lips traveled across my shoulder blades and down my spine, and I shivered from the feel of his hot mouth on my skin. I was so desperate to be inside him, to feel his body constrict around my cock, to experience all of him.

Is that how he felt as well?

When his lips made their way to the waistband of my briefs, he curled his fingers inside, slowing tugging my underwear down my cheeks. I felt the air hit my skin, and it soothed the prickling heat racing along my back.

Following the descent of the material, he kissed my skin inch by inch before finally yanking my underwear off of my legs. I trembled, feeling completely exposed but also extremely turned on.

I waited for that small tremor of fear that would spiral through me when Jake would be entirely too rough, topping me when I was high as a kite. I felt nearly indefensible when I was with him, mostly because of the drugs, but also because he'd become so unpredictable in his behavior.

But with Vaughn I felt safe and cared for. His warm mouth skimmed over my ass before kissing lower to my inner thighs, and for the first time in years, I considered wanting more.

When he parted my cheeks and blew on my hole, I nearly sprang off the bed. "What the fuck are you doing?"

"Just relax and let me explore. I know you've got your reasons for not wanting to be fucked, and I have a good idea what they might be, but Christ, can you please trust me?" he said in a growl. "I've got needs too. And right now I need to make you feel good."

I fell silent and slackened into his touch as he continued to lick, nip, and blow cool air on my thighs and cheeks. I squirmed and groaned, ready to fucking explode.

"Is...is this enough for you?" I whispered. What in the hell was I asking?

"You mean being a bottom?" he asked, as if he could read my every thought. "Goddamn, Reed."

He angled my head and slid his lips tenderly against mine, his tongue dipping inside my mouth. Nothing felt better than kissing him. Nothing.

"Listen," he said, his eyes connecting with mine. "I'll take anything I can get when it comes to you. You got me so cranked up. Lately, all I can think about is your cock in my ass."

I inhaled a sharp breath. Those words made my chest feel tight and funny.

"Same here," I admitted, stroking my thumb across his cheek.

"Sure, I'm used to topping, and I fantasize about what it'd feel like to be inside you. But I get it," he said low in my ear. "For now, let me play."

His fingers slid up to dig into my back as he kissed open-mouthed between my shoulder blades. When his hands kneaded lower to my cheeks, I moaned. My fingers tightened around my balls to keep myself from exploding.

"I don't want you getting your needs met anywhere else," I said, panting. "Not while you're with me."

He hummed in response. The heels of his hands nudged my cheeks open, and the tip of his tongue traced my hole. Jesus fuck, I almost shot to the ceiling.

"I don't want anybody else, Reed." I dug my head into the pillow and groaned.

When he blew across my sensitive tissue, my cock swelled even further.

"I need to taste you." His slick and gentle tongue licked. His cool breath puffed softly on my skin. "You got your turn. Now let me have mine, yeah?"

I let him have me because I was so completely gone for him, I wanted more. I arched my ass as he kissed and licked at my hole, my entire body vibrating as pinpricks of heat swept across my skin. I was moving my hips in a messy, jagged pattern, already a shuddering mess before his tongue pressed inside.

I whimpered, which practically turned into a sob, because it was the most amazing sensation, allowing him that intimacy.

"Christ," he said. "You are so sexy here. If this is the only way I can get inside you...fuck."

His thumbs spread my hole open, and he dipped his tongue between my inner walls, moaning as if he was just as turned on. A long and low groan released from my throat as his tongue jabbed and wormed its way inside.

As if he could reach that other battered place as well. The one with the stitched-up pieces. Tattered and worn, having suffered long and hard to make it out of a dark and shadowy past.

I felt gutless, unable to move my limbs or breathe, for that matter, the air leeching out of me with every gasp. His finger replaced his tongue, and at first it felt so foreign, I winced and squirmed. But then he gave his wrist a twist and hit that spot inside me that I had nearly forgotten existed. Another quick stroke and stars floated in front of my eyes. Everything buzzed awake inside me. I was in a supreme state of euphoria.

"Uuuuuuhhhh, Vaughn." He was finger fucking me now, and I was moving my hips to match his rhythm. I could almost imagine his cock pushing inside me, and it made me nearly feverish. He wouldn't be rough unless I requested it. More than likely, he'd feel amazing.

"You like that?"

"Hell yes, but I...I'm about to lose my fucking mind."

He removed his fingers and I immediately mourned the loss. "Turn over."

My limbs felt rubbery as I flipped to my back. My cock curved against my stomach, full and leaking. He looked down at my length as if in awe and reached across the nightstand for a condom and some lube.

He suited me up and then applied lube generously before finally straddling me. He grazed my lips and slowly lowered himself on top. My fingers gripped his thighs as my cock breached his tight hole. He stilled as I whimpered, barely hanging on.

"Damn, you're a sight for sore eyes," I said. His cock was long and beautiful, his chest flushed, and his mouth gleaming wet from being inside me.

"I'm not going to last."

He grabbed his cock, fondling it in long and easy strokes, knowing exactly how he liked it. My hand wrapped around his and he bowed his back, urging me on, as I pumped him good and fast.

"I need you to move, Vaughn."

He nodded in understanding, lifting his ass and slamming back down, while his fist gripped his length. "Christ."

My balls were tight and my spine was hot and prickling. He threw his head back and lost it, his come surging onto my stomach and chest and neck. A glob landed on my lip and I licked it off, groaning and tasting him.

I clutched his muscular thighs and thrust upward, feeling his hot hole contract around me. A couple of drives more and I broke completely apart, shooting load after load inside him, bent on finding my salvation.

I was trembling from head to toe, my heart thrashing in my chest, and he wrapped his limbs around me, tucking his head into my neck. "Fuck, that was—"

He licked a trail up my neck, attempting to rein in his breaths.

Several minutes later, when he could finally move, he disposed of the condom and cleaned us both up, using his T-shirt from the floor.

"Stay in my bed tonight." I pulled him back into my arms. "Every night."

I liked the weight of him on top of me, our soft cocks brushing alongside each other. His breath on my neck, his soft hair on my cheek.

"You sure?"

"Never been more sure," I said and he hummed, licking a stripe beneath my ear.

The smaller black cat bolted inside the room and jumped on the end of the bed, curling herself into a tight ball. The gray feline followed suit, kneading the comforter and then bending himself against the other cat.

Vaughn smiled lazily. "Guess they like the idea, too."

Our lips met again and we explored each other's mouths, tongue to tongue, breath to breath, until he rolled over and we fell into a deep and sated sleep.

CHAPTER TWENTY-SIX
VAUGHN

We relaxed into an almost natural routine the next couple of days, and I got a taste of what it might've been like having a partner, another person to come home to day in and day out. Maybe a sample of what Jude and Cory's life was like. I tried not to think too hard about how much I liked it, looked forward to it even.

I wanted Smoke, needed to be in his bed. Not only to have him fuck me into the mattress but also to feel the warmth and security of his arms. That mix of cinnamon and brine, spice and salt, that always greeted me when I inhaled him, tasted his neck. I craved that look in his eyes when he was inside me. Maybe that had been my first mistake, to always search for something in his gaze.

But whatever I was looking for, I found it, even if it would never be voiced out loud. I was in love with Smoke, and I wasn't sure if the feeling was mutual, but given the tenderness I consistently felt from him, it might've been close.

And it was so fucked up, because I was staying with him to keep myself safe but also to try to draw out the guy who was fucking with me. And each night I wanted Jake to show himself to the club, and not, all at the same time.

Because then this temporary arrangement with Smoke would end. And it would be time. To man up. To make a decision about who we were to each other and what we wanted. We couldn't be on hold forever.

Today was my day off, Mal had invited me to the compound for a barbeque, and I had accepted. But first I needed to visit my dad. Smoke and I were driving up together, and he would be meeting me at my pop's house after working for a bit at the auto parts store.

I arrived to find Mary, the home health nurse, sitting with him. "Is he still being ornery?"

"Of course." She grinned. "I wouldn't have him any other way."

"You see? I haven't been a problem," Dad said with a scowl on his face. But I also saw something else alight in his eyes when he looked her way. Huh. Did my pop have a crush on Mary?

She was an attractive woman, with shoulder-length reddish hair and a nice figure. She also looked to be about ten years younger than my pop.

She removed the blood pressure cuff and was about to place the thermometer in his mouth. "Now keep that trap closed so I can take your temperature and speak to your son."

He grumbled something as she slipped the plastic stick beneath his tongue. She rolled her eyes but also smiled warmly at him. I could tell he enjoyed the attention, and much like my stepmother would dote on him, Mary seemed to be overly accommodating as well. I was only now putting the pieces together. How she stayed longer than expected and baked him oatmeal raisin cookies last week. Go figure.

"All his vital signs have been good," she said, giving him a pointed look to keep his lips sealed. He seemed to like her sass but would probably never admit to it out loud. "He just needs to add more vegetables and exercise to his routine."

"Good luck with that," he said once she removed the thermometer.

"I'll somehow wrangle you into going for a short stroll with me in a couple of days," she said in a teasing tone as their eyes caught and held. I had to look away. Didn't matter how old I was, my father turning on the charm wasn't something I wanted to witness.

"A couple of days, huh? So you're giving me a break tomorrow?" Pop asked. He almost looked like a pouty little kid. I hid my smirk with a cough.

"My coworker will be taking over my shift, so you better be nice," she teased as my dad's shoulders practically slumped in disappointment. "My son and his boyfriend have a layover tomorrow, and I want to spend a few hours with them before they leave for their Hawaiian vacation."

Pop's mouth contorted as if he's swallowed a lemon drop. To make up for his rudeness, I stepped up to the plate. "That sounds real nice. I've always wanted to visit Hawaii."

She nodded. "My late husband and I always gushed about how much we loved it there, so I guess my son had a little influence."

I nodded. "Well if you need a casual place for an early dinner, you can always stop into the Hog's Den. The late afternoons are quiet, and the tab would be on me."

"I appreciate that. Your dad always tells me you're a stand-up guy," she said, patting my arm and waving goodbye. Pop watched the doorway a little too long after she left, as if hoping she'd magically reappear. I almost ribbed him a little about Mary, but I didn't want him to clam up on me. Embarrassing or not, it was nice to see that light in his eyes again.

"What's your deal?" I asked as his silence continued.

"Nothing, I guess…" he sighed. "That didn't surprise you?"

"Which part?" I said, bracing the counter.

"That she spoke about her gay son like it was no big thing," he said.

"Maybe because it *ain't* no big thing."

He stared at me, his eyebrows arching together. "When I was coming up—"

"Maybe people should be free to love whoever and however they want," I said, unable to stop myself. "And it shouldn't be anybody's business."

"You saying you accept that kind of lifestyle?"

"Let's put it this way. Obviously Mary's son felt comfortable enough to come out to his mother, and she sounds like she still loves and accepts him fully." I felt my chest tighten up. "Now it might've been tough for her at first—you never know unless you ask—but the place she's at with him now? Sounds pretty damn cool."

I snatched a glass from the cupboard and filled it with water, my throat feeling awfully parched. I gulped a little and then turned back to him. "You telling me that if your child confessed the same, you'd disown him or stop loving him? After losing Leanne the way you did, don't you think life is too short for that kind of bullshit?"

His eyes grew shiny at the mention of my stepmom, and I felt like shit for making him emotional. But this was the kind of conversation I'd always avoided with him. It was just something we never discussed. So maybe having somebody like Mary in his life was good, if only for a while.

We watched a little television, and then I made him some soup with his favorite oyster crackers. I stared at the clock above his head. It was in the shape of a giant coffee cup, one that you'd see at a small, out-of-the-way diner or something.

He followed my gaze and a ghost of a smile lined his lips. "That one is Mary's favorite."

"Somebody's got it bad," I said, before I could take it back.

"What are you—"

"Don't even try to deny it," I said. "It's all cool. Maybe when you go for your walk, it should be to a flea market. You're due for a new clock, yeah?"

He narrowed his eyes. "I thought you said my clocks were a pain in the ass."

"They are." I stood up rinse our bowls. "But it would nice to have somebody to share your interests with."

Pop's face looked momentarily conflicted as he drummed his fingers on the tabletop. I leaned closer to him and whispered, "I think Leanne would approve."

"Mary's my nurse," he sputtered. "I'm sure there's some code or another about not crossing any lines."

I folded my arms across my chest and studied him. "Maybe so. But if it's mutual, you'll figure it out together. For now, enjoy the company."

He nodded, and I grabbed my phone to check my messages. Just as I was wondering what was taking Smoke so long, there was a rumble of noise in the driveway and then a knock on the door a minute later.

"C'mon in," I said.

Smoke pushed open the screen and strolled inside, one hand in the back pocket of his tight jeans, a bandana tied around his head. His high cheekbones looked flushed from the wind and damn, those plump, rosy lips were tempting. Fuck me.

His eyes latched onto mine, and we soaked each other in as if we hadn't seen each other in days. Pop cleared his throat and I shook my head, cursing at myself for looking like a lovesick puppy myself.

"Pop," I said, swallowing thickly. "You remember—"

"Reed," he said, holding out his hand. Smoke's cheeks colored even further.

"Mr. O'Keefe," Smoke said, shaking his hand before his gaze darted to the wall behind him. "Whoa. Vaughn told me you had quite a collection, but I didn't picture all of this."

"Some crazy shit, right?" I said, almost laughing at Smoke's wigged out expression.

I watched him in awe as he walked around the room, admiring the clocks from different angles. At first I thought maybe he was only acting impressed to make my pop feel good, but after a couple minutes more, I wasn't so sure.

"This one looks like it was made from a heavy-duty sheet of chrome from the late…what would you say?" he asked, looking over at my dad. It was a retro-looking clock with beige and eggshell-blue coloring.

"Vintage 1950s," Dad said without even a pause. "Dealer said that particular shipment came from France."

"France, huh?" Smoke said, his fingers curling over the arch. "Fancy."

After a few more minutes of listening to the two of them shoot the breeze about different metal compounds and treatments, I was itching to hightail it out of there and get on the road.

I hadn't told my dad that I'd been staying with Smoke; there was no need to worry him. But after our heavy conversation earlier, it was time he finally knew some other things about me.

Soon, I told myself. Besides, he was just getting to know Smoke, and he seemed to like him. Having Smoke here with me felt promising, and I'd hate for him to think that he wasn't welcome anymore. Who knew how my dad would respond?

"We should probably get going." I bit down on my lip, not wanting it to seem like I was in a rush. But I was definitely looking forward to our ride.

Smoke looked over at me, his eyes snagging on my mouth.

"How'd you get that scar, anyway?" he asked suddenly.

"This one?" I rubbed my finger over the jagged flesh. I knew exactly what he was referring to after his teeth and lips and tongue had smoothed over it too many times to count.

"It was from that broken bottle in the backyard, right?" my pop suddenly chimed in. "He and his friend Z were always goofing off and getting into trouble."

"BB gun incident?" Smoke asked, as if he hadn't heard all my ridiculous stories at the bar a thousand times over by now.

"Yup," I said. "Gave my pop and my stepmom a run for their money."

"So I've heard," Smoke said, crossing his arms, a wistful smile on his face.

I shook my head and then patted Pop on the back. "You know to call if you need me, right?"

"Of course," he said, stretching his legs out on his ottoman. He looked over at Smoke standing beside me. "You come visit anytime, son."

Smoke signaled a goodbye with his hand. "I'd like that, sir."

CHAPTER TWENTY-SEVEN
VAUGHN

We stepped inside the compound only to discover that most everybody was hanging out back on this sunny day. Jonas was manning the grill while his old lady stood next to him, chatting up some other girlfriends and wives.

I didn't allow my gaze to linger on Smoke longer than necessary as he walked away to pick up a game of cornhole out on the sprawling lawn. Who would've thought a bunch of tough-as-nails bikers were capable of being so domestic?

I took a seat at one of the long wooden benches and grabbed some pretzels from the bowl in the middle of the table. Though I could be overly talkative in my own establishment, out here some might consider me the exact opposite. Not that I didn't feel welcome. Just didn't feel like myself, at least not lately. Like I was keeping a secret so large, I would break apart any moment. All the stripped-down pieces of myself would float away in the wind.

I'd realized these past weeks how much of myself I'd been hiding. I was a man who enjoyed the company of both men and women. When I was with a lady, nobody batted an eye, not even my pop. Because it was considered normal.

No guy had ever really kept my interest for long, not outside of mutual attraction or sex. Not like how Smoke had captured me—heart and soul. He was the first man—the first person—I could actually envision a future with. One whom I desperately wanted as part of my life on a daily basis, and that thought alone was making me feel restless and twitchy.

Not because it would be denying or quieting that other part of myself. My attraction to women would always remain. Didn't mean I needed or wanted to screw them all. It meant that from out of the fire that burned deep in my core, Smoke turned out to be the darkest flame. Just one look and he utterly consumed me.

But now more than ever I was faced with exposing the part of myself that might change how others viewed me. It wasn't so much that I was scared, because fuck, I could clearly take care of myself. Even my pop would come around eventually, I hoped.

It was that I felt a sense of responsibility to these men who were keeping me safe. I wasn't being up front with them, but here I was, sitting in their house—eating their food, drinking their beer—and they didn't even know the real reason why they were providing me a safe harbor.

"You good, Vaughn?" I heard a familiar feminine voice over my shoulder. Already Melanie had sought me out.

"Yeah, how about yourself?" She handed me a beer and I accepted it gratefully, since I hadn't yet reached for one in the cooler.

I certainly didn't want a repeat of our last time in the back bedroom, so I simply smiled politely, then turned my attention to the recruit who had sat down next to me.

Felix lived below Smoke, and from what I could tell, they seemed to be pretty tight. But I couldn't say I'd ever had a real conversation with the man outside of the bar.

Melanie patted my shoulder and then took a seat on the other side of me to speak with one of the ladies across the table. When I knew for certain she was engaged in the other conversation, I again turned my attention to Felix. "You seen anything out there on patrol?"

He looked over his shoulder to gauge whether or not anybody was listening. "I saw someone poking around in your lot last night. I gave chase but he got away."

My back went rigid. Had Jake broken into my apartment for a third time? At this point, I felt like torching the place down and starting over from scratch.

I didn't know how I was going to feel comfortable enough to make a life there for myself again.

"Think he got inside?" I asked, almost afraid of the answer. Nothing that was left there was valuable to me. It was more the intent that boiled my blood.

"Pretty unlikely," he said. "Looked like he was just pulling in. By the time I got around the corner, he'd already heard my motor and gunned it out of there."

"What would've happened had you caught up to him?" I asked real low, so nobody grasped onto our conversation.

Felix's dark brown eyes bored into mine as if he was debating whether or not to share the plain truth. "I'd bring him to Mal."

The statement was simple, but also held a hint of danger and intrigue. It reminded me whom I was dealing with here. The Disciples might have been having a barbeque on their spacious property in the country, but they never let down their guard.

"And then what?" I muttered. "He brings his own form of justice?"

He shifted his weight to turn toward me. As if to school me on the politics of biker clubs. "Mal believes in having proof and until he sees it for himself, he's not going to take out another club member on speculation alone."

My stomach rumbled thinking about just how Jake would've been taken out. Still, Mal was a smart and sound leader. I sipped from my beer to cover my hesitancy. "Sound decision."

Felix's gaze followed mine to Smoke on the back lawn. He had his arm around one of the biker babes and though I kept my features neutral, for a moment I thought I had been busted. My mouth opened to make some kind of flippant remark about him getting laid. But Felix beat me to the punch.

"You've been a sport about all of this."

"It's no real hardship," I said after dragging my lips away from the bottle. "Smoke's a good guy letting me stay at his place."

"That he is," he said and then wiggled his eyebrows as the girl whispered something in Smoke's ear. "If he keeps you up tonight, hope he makes it up to you somehow."

I laughed and nearly choked on another swig, hoping the acid sloshing around in my stomach didn't come up my throat. It looked like Felix wanted to say something else, but he held himself back.

The girl kissed Smoke's cheek, and I felt a pang of jealousy flare up. Smoke's head drew back, and his fiery gaze connected so solidly with mine that right then I knew with crystal clear certainty that he wouldn't be going home with anybody else but me. Thump. Thump. Thump.

This was for show, and I had to be okay with that, for now, so I focused my eyes on the grill, where Jonas was lip-locked with his old lady.

Felix made a noise in the back of his throat as the backyard grew eerily silent. A couple of Scorpions had showed up, proudly wearing their leather cuts and bandanas. I recognized only Fish, who stood with two of his men flanked on either side.

The quiet continued to draw out until Mal strode from the back table, where he had been holding court with some ladies.

"Welcome," he hollered by way of greeting, lifting his beer bottle.

Like a skipped record that had been placed back on track, the noise rushed back in again, and some of the Disciples stepped forward to greet the newcomers. I watched as Felix sauntered over to clap one of the club members on the back. Fish stood talking to Mal.

The dude on the other side of Fish made eye contact with me and held steady. Then his gaze traveled down my torso, as if he were checking me out, maybe even eye-fucking me. Either that or I was losing it. I felt a delicate hand on my thigh and realized that Melanie had turned toward me. I resisted pulling away lest this guy see straight through me. I had zero interest in Melanie, let alone any other woman or man. I only had eyes for one person at this party.

Next thing I knew, Smoke had materialized directly in front of me, as if he had read my thoughts or was attempting to block the guy's view.

"Hey, Vaughn," he said nervously, which was so unlike him. "Any more of those brews left in the cooler?"

"Uh," I said, nearly struck dumb, because it sounded like a fake conversation. Smoke didn't even drink alcohol. I looked over at Melanie, who had been the one to grab the beer in the first place, and raised my bottle.

"I'm not sure," she said. "But I'd be happy to check for you."

"Thanks, honey," Smoke said as she sashayed by him. His gaze immediately fell back to mine again.

"Who is that?" I asked, knowing he'd understand full well whom I was referring to.

"One of Fish's recruits," he said. "Guy by the name of Sawyer."

"You think he suspects something?" I said low and steady.

"He always eyeballs me when I'm there, makes me nervous," he said. "Don't know what he's playing at or if he's only feeling us out, seeing who might be interested, if you know what I mean."

"Sure seems that way to me." I avoided looking in his direction again so he didn't figure out we were talking about him.

"But tonight it seems like he's checking *you* out," Smoke said through gritted teeth. "And I don't like it."

Hearing the jealousy in his voice made the blood thrum wildly in my veins.

"Why would he be so obvious about it?" I asked.

"Is it really noticeable to anybody else, though?"

I looked around the crowd, most of whom were either well on their way to being smashed or completely unaware of us at the moment. "I guess not."

A large hand clapped Smoke's back, and he flinched. It was Fish. "Hey, Smoke, you having a good time?"

"Yeah, for sure," he said, shaking Fish's hand. The guy who'd been eye-fucking me earlier suddenly had an entrance, and he sidled up next to Fish.

"I haven't met you before," he said, reaching out his hand. "I'm Sawyer."

I stretched my arm, and his clammy palm clasped onto mine. "Vaughn."

"You manage the Hog's Den, right?" His hand lingered on mine, and even from my side view, I could see the vein in Smoke's temple throbbing.

"Right," I said, sliding my fingers away and swigging my beer.

He looked around at his boss, who was busy talking to Felix.

He cocked an eyebrow. "Anyone single at this party or is everybody taken?"

I clenched my jaw tight to prevent a reaction as he blatantly stared me down. Holy fuck was that a forward move.

"Who exactly do you have your eye on?" Smoke said through a clenched jaw.

"I'm single, honey," Melanie said, stepping forward with Smoke's beer. For the first time tonight, I was relieved to see her.

"Are you now, sugar?' Sawyer drawled and then thumped me on the shoulder. "I figured you were with Vaughn here."

"I'm not with anybody," she said and then looked pointedly at me. "Isn't that right, baby?"

Sawyer looked between the two of us. "Maybe Vaughn wanted you for himself tonight?"

I found it hard to swallow. Smoke's gaze burned into me, but I couldn't meet his eyes.

"We made no plans," Melanie said, running a finger down Sawyer's arm. "But he can join us if he wants."

Sawyer's eyes latched onto mine as if silently pleading with me to accept the offer. And maybe any other time I would've. But not when the man I desperately wanted to be with was standing right beside him. And I couldn't even let the world know.

I wanted to grab Smoke by the neck and haul him toward me, kiss him hard, and ask him to take me home. The tension coiled around us like a lasso, and I felt the hairs on my arms rise as his elbow brushed innocently against mine.

"Nah, not tonight." I attempted to look natural when I was strung so damn tight, he could've played me like a fiddle. "You guys enjoy yourselves."

I turned away and walked back inside the compound, tucking my shaking hands inside my pockets.

I'd been propositioned by guys before, but not in this environment. I wasn't sure what the hell was happening, but something felt way off. It was as if the world had gone and turned itself upside down.

I stayed inside for a bit, shooting the breeze with a couple other Disciples, and Smoke smartly chose not to follow. I wasn't sure what ended up happening dbetween Melanie and Sawyer, but after another hour, I texted Smoke that I was taking off.

Smoke: About fucking time. Right behind you.

CHAPTER TWENTY-EIGHT
SMOKE

Vaughn was barely inside the door before I was caging him against the wall. "I want you to fuck me."

I felt his cock tighten in his pants as my lips stroked against his. "Does this have anything to do with the proposition I received tonight?"

"Maybe, maybe not. Does it really matter?" I asked, my lips pressed against his neck. "Point is, I'm not sure how much time I've got with you. It kills me to think of you topping some other guy, and I…"

"You what?" he said, shoving at my shoulders in frustration, but I refused to budge. I didn't want to be away from him for even one moment longer. "I already told you, I'll take what I can get."

"I want you to own me," I said, biting at a patch of skin at the hollow of his throat, and I felt him shiver. "I need to feel you inside me, in case…"

"What?" Vaughn said, challenging me again. He doubted whether I was thinking clearly. He didn't want me to have any regrets. Little did he realize I'd never been more sure. "You don't have to prove anything to me."

"You need me to spell it out?" I asked, thrusting my hips against his groin, showing him how fucking much I needed him. "I've never felt this way before, okay? So consumed by somebody. Like I want to—"

He waited me out, his gaze scorching into mine. I saw the same thing reflected back at me, so I knew I was safe to tell him how I felt. I'd tell him even if I were still uncertain of his feelings. I was tired of holding it all inside.

I grasped at his face and then gentled my mouth against his lips. "Fuck, Vaughn, I feel like I want you here with me always. I…I'm in love with you."

His entire body pulled taut as a fishing line and for a split second, I thought I had said the wrong thing.

Until he growled and flipped me around, shoving me hard against the wall. "Jesus fuck, Reed. That's all I've been feeling for days on end."

My heart clawed its way up my throat as I gaped at him. He had my hand locked above my head, and all I wanted to do was submit to him. Get down on my knees and worship him.

"Goddamn it," he said, his lips raining kisses over my chin, my cheeks, and each of my eyelids, while I tried governing my runaway breaths. "I'm head over heels for you, man. I don't want to be with anybody else. You're it for me."

My heart nearly exploded out of my chest as I clutched at his neck and crashed my mouth against his. My fingertips pressed against the pulse at his neck, which was fluttering as erratically as mine.

We left a trail of clothing in the hallway leading to the bed. I was trembling with untapped energy but also undeniable panic. I was finally allowing somebody inside. Somebody I was in love with.

Fuck, I was in so deep with him. And I'd just told him so.

Vaughn pressed me facedown on the bed and his lips were everywhere. On my ear and neck, shoulders and back, licking and biting and marking me. Making me his. And fuck, that was all I wanted right then. To be his, only his.

I squashed down that little voice in the back of my head urging me to fight back, to force him off me. But this was Vaughn. He wasn't going to mistreat me. He'd even stop if I asked him to.

When I angled my head, he took my mouth, and we warred it out with our tongues. His fingers clutched the back of my neck and he tugged at my hair, commanding the kiss, taking what he wanted. Then he reached for the lube, and within a few seconds his finger was pushing at my hole.

I immediately tensed, and his gaze shot to mine. His finger slid out of me, almost remorsefully. But I gripped the sheet in front of me. "No. Please. Again."

I felt him exhale against my back. I didn't want him to give up so easily.

First one finger, then two. He was inside me, and I was pushing back against his hand. As he scissored his digits back and forth, the span felt uncomfortable and sucked the breath right out of me.

In another minute, the muscle loosened as if from memory, and the pain transformed to ripples of pleasure.

He nudged my shoulder to the mattress, his lips on the small of my back, while his fingers curved upward and worked their magic. "Tell me you want this, Reed."

Vaughn using my real name during sex gave my heart a jolt. I looked back at him as my hips continued moving against his hand. "Fuck yes. I need you now."

When he ripped open the condom wrapper, I stilled, but my cock was throbbing against the mattress. His hips tentatively slid against mine, his large cock gently prodding at my crease, and I held my breath.

"Just do it," I bit out, unsure of why he was hesitating.

"When I'm good and ready," he grunted and grasped at my jaw, planting a bruising kiss on my nape. Letting me know exactly who was in charge. He was essentially telling me to give up control, and I was more than ready to hand it all to him.

"You got it, Boss," I said. He stiffened and let out a deep growl. The last time I'd called him that was our first day together behind the bar. He slid his broad cock down the crack of my ass and barely breeched my snug hole.

"Fuck," I shouted, and I heard a gurgled response as his fingers clamped hard around my hips. He became motionless as he rested his head against my shoulder blade, and I could feel the warm air releasing from his lips.

"You okay?" he whispered, as if afraid even to move a muscle. Vaughn's cock felt fucking huge, and it stung like hell, but I nodded anyway, because I remembered what was yet to come.

As I became adjusted to his girth, he drove forward another inch, and there it was, the pleasure-pain that I once seemed to crave.

Before other shit ruined the experience for me.

"Uuuuhhhh, you're so damn tight," he said, and he thrust further inside. "Goddamn, that's—"

I fisted the covers because the sensation was too much for my brain to handle. I moaned and swayed my hips, nearly toppling to the side and hunching in a ball. His arm reached down to hook around my abdomen and he kept me tucked up against him.

He kissed my shoulder, bit it on a growl, and then began moving. Shallow stabs at first, but enough to make me shudder and sweat.

"Damn, it's good," he said. "So fucking good. Like nothing else."

His talking had always been arousing, but while he was buried balls-deep inside me? Amazingly fucking hot.

"Come on, Vaughn, give me more of that incredible cock," I said, driving back into his length. "I can take it."

His hands grabbed onto my ass cheeks and squeezed as if my challenge had provided him a renewed energy. His hips propelled haphazardly against me, and thrust after thrust sent me spiraling higher. My balls began tingling, and I sank down on my forearms, groaning long and low.

His chest dropped against my back. It felt so nice to have his skin next to mine, like we were one unit, working toward the same satisfying goal.

"Fuck, Reed, I can't even—" He slowed his hips and laid sloppy kisses on my shoulder and neck. "Turn over. *Now*."

His tone was so strained, so persuasive, that I heeded his command. He pulled out momentarily as I flipped myself onto my back, and before I could feel the loss he was back inside. My knees were hiked up to my shoulders.

And fuck, seeing his glazed eyes, the blissed out expression on his face, was so gratifying. Intense. Beautiful.

He leaned down and offered me a tender kiss, his softened gaze on mine the entire time. Our mouths touched and lingered, breathing the same air. I gently sucked on his lip before he lifted up, his arms quivering.

"Reed," he croaked out the moment before he began pounding me into the bed. A shudder quaked through me. I would feel his thick cock filling me, stretching me, all the way into next month, but I fucking loved it.

I loved that he could give me exactly what I wanted. And what he so desperately needed.

A flush of color moved across his cheeks, then down his chest, and his hands forced my thighs even higher. The sound emitting from deep in his throat was driving me wild. My mouth opened in a silent chant as my eyes practically rolled in the back of my head.

"Goddamn, you're incredible." His fist closed around my cock.

He began stroking me in time with his thrusts, and within seconds I blew apart in his hand. My orgasm was so intense that everything went white. Even the sound had been blunted. And just as I was attempting to gain a firm grasp back on the planet, his balls were slapping into my flesh, he was growling, and he came with a shout.

"Uuuuuuuhh, fuck," he groaned and fell on top of me, panting into my neck.

We didn't move for several long moments, and though he was heavy against my limbs, I felt sated, happy, free. *Alive.*

Finally he sank down beside me on the bed and pulled me into his arms. He kissed me on the side of my head. "Fuck, I could get used to that."

"Don't get any bright ideas," I mumbled into his chest, and the deep rumble of his laugh made my heart clench tight.

"Thank you," he said, licking a stripe up my neck.

"What for?" I looked up at him through slits. I was so drowsy.

"I know that was a big deal for you," he said, his fingers twining through my hair. "I'm no idiot."

"Glad it was *you*, Vaughn," I mumbled, and he inhaled deeply, bringing me further into the warmth of his arms.

After several more minutes of short kisses and fingernails tracing over skin, he rolled off the bed to dispose of the condom and returned with a warm washcloth.

I reached for the rag, but he resisted. "Let me."

I sank onto my back and as he wiped off our chests and stomachs, I watched his fingers circling gently over my skin.

"I've been thinking about how we can make this work," I said in a tentative voice.

His hand froze on my chest. "What do you mean?"

"You and me." He stared into my eyes for a long moment, his gaze alight with opposing emotions—hope and trepidation and affection.

He lay down beside me. "You realize we haven't even been on a date, like real people."

I jerked my shoulder. "I don't give a fuck about coming out to anybody, if that's what you mean."

"What I mean is that this can never be normal, not in our world," he said. "You're the one who has everything to lose."

"You have a business," I said, laying my head against his neck. "You don't think that's huge?"

"Sure, but I can go anywhere and open a bar," he said, burrowing his fingers in my scalp. "You have a brotherhood you've sworn to. A life with the Disciples."

"Yeah, sure," I said. "But I never found anybody I wanted to lose everything for."

He grabbed the back of my head and hauled my mouth to his. His lips fused onto mine, and his tongue delved deep inside my mouth. The kiss was desperate and filled with unspoken things. Promises, hopes, and dreams.

When our lips broke apart, he panted into my mouth. "Fuck. You make me want things that I never really had. Never thought I wanted before."

I pulled his bottom lip into my mouth and sucked softly on it until he groaned. "Sometimes I just wish…"

He gave me a lingering kiss. "Wish what?"

"That it were different," I whispered into his neck. "Just you and me and the bar, a more quiet life." I thought about the sound of the glasses clanging, the tap foaming, the hum of the crowd, the woodsy scent of the tables and bar top when you stepped inside the door. It smelled and sounded so familiar, so comforting.

Vaughn lay completely still beside me, and I could hear his uneven breaths. What I envisioned wasn't even close to the same thing he had going with that fucker who had invested in his bar and then left him high and dry. I wanted to share everything with this man.

"You know," I said, "there was a time I thought I'd inherit my family's business and do my metal pieces on the side."

"What about the club?" Vaughn's voice was low and scratchy.

"Dunno. Think maybe I needed that stability and support in my life," I said, confessing my deepest secrets. "But I question whether I need it anymore."

"You're fucking serious right now, aren't you?" He sat up and grabbed my chin. "By screwing around with me, you suddenly realized all this?"

I tried to shake from his grasp. "Christ, you make it sound like—"

I pushed out of his arms and swung my legs over the side of the bed. This was a mistake. My stomach was in knots. What had I been thinking?

"Wait." Vaughn's strong arm reached around my waist, and he tugged me back into his arms. I could've resisted, but I let him manhandle me. "Fuck, I'm sorry. I just...I don't want to be the reason why you gave something up in your life."

"Not giving something up." I rushed my fingers through my hair in frustration. "Gaining something."

"Hell, Reed," he said, feathering kisses across my shoulders and neck. "This is some scary shit. I already had somebody who skirted town on me and—"

"I get it, okay?" I said, unwilling to make eye contact.

"It would never be like that. *Never.* Fuck, I'm putting it on the line. Would be nice to know what you're feeling, too." Vaughn nudged my jawline in order to meet my eyes. His gaze was so penetrating and intense; I thought maybe he was never going to respond. My throat was tight as my heart lodged solidly in place.

"Sometimes I—" he whispered in a choked voice. "I want to be with you so fucking bad I can hardly breathe."

I closed my eyes and shuddered out a breath. Ah, hell.

"Afraid to imagine a life with you," he said, his mouth against my lips. "Don't want the rug pulled from under me."

"I hear you," I said, rubbing my scruff against his. "Just a stupid pipe dream anyway. I got no money of my own, only a club that relies on me, and I'm basically shitting on them right now."

"Hey, that's not true," he said. "You're only trying to figure out your life. That ain't nothing to be ashamed of."

We lay silent for a long time, each lost in our own heads. I shifted so that our legs were tangled together beneath the covers.

"Tell me what you're thinking," I mumbled before drifting off.

"About you and me," he said in a groggy voice, repositioning his arm beneath my shoulder. "Never want to let you go."

CHAPTER TWENTY-NINE
VAUGHN

It was after hours at the bar. Lewis and Cherry had already gone home. That was exactly where I wanted to be with Smoke. Behind closed doors where I could touch him freely. Sleep naked beside him.

Earlier in the evening, Mal and Jonas had held a back room meeting, and the Disciples came away buzzing. Something was up. I could see it in their hardened posture, in their watchful gaze.

"What's going on?" I had asked Smoke on one of his passes behind me at the bar. I wouldn't normally inquire about Disciples business, but I had a feeling it might be something directly affecting me. I already knew our arrangement might be coming to an end, no matter how accustomed I'd become to sharing Smoke's bed.

"Can't give details. But the Asylum is going down. Should all be over in a couple days' time," he muttered.

My breath had caught in my lungs. I wasn't sure I was comfortable having information that huge. But it wasn't like I didn't know it was imminent. Word on the street was that the Asylum had it coming. They had screwed over far too many clubs.

Depending on how crippled the Asylum became, I only hoped that Jake had more important things to think about than whom Smoke was fucking.

I'd be free to move back to my apartment or find a new one, more than likely. Guess I should've started looking. That thought sat heavy in my gut.

Sure, Smoke and I had confessed our dreams and desires to each other the other night. But the following day, the reality of the situation merely came crashing back in. Neither of us had brought it up again.

Smoke had a bug up his ass the last couple of days anyhow, after he'd spotted Fish and Sawyer out at the compound one afternoon. Sawyer had barely made eye contact this time, and it had made Smoke super anxious. When he brought Sawyer up to Mal, Mal vouched for him through and through.

I grabbed the bin of dirty glasses from beneath the bar and headed to the kitchen to run them through the washer. Smoke reached for the full trash can at his end to empty in the Dumpster out back.

Smoke approached me from behind and pulled me into a scorching kiss. "I haven't been able to do that all day."

"After this week—"

"Don't even say it," he said, tapping his lips to mine. "We'll figure it out and make a decision together. I just want to enjoy you right now."

He had me backed against the cold metal freezer, his lips at my neck, and I groaned as his mouth pulled delicately at my skin. His stubble was prickling my collarbone, and my fingers worked through his hair.

"Let's take this home," Smoke said, his fingers tracing along my chin.

Home. That word falling from his lips sounded so right. I closed my eyes against the panic welling inside me over having all of this end.

"Shit!" I heard from the doorway, and my heart made a free fall to my stomach. We both looked up at the same time as Felix shuffled awkwardly backward, his body half turned as if ready to bolt. "I just...sorry... didn't mean..."

He was as much at a loss for words as we were. Smoke took a step away from me, and I felt the loss of heat immediately as a cold dread set up shop in my gut.

"Wait," Smoke said, ripping his shaky hands through his hair. "Let me explain."

"No, it's all cool." Felix help up his hands to stave him off. "It actually makes a fuck ton of sense now."

I could barely look at him, so Smoke did the talking. "What does?"

"Why that fucker has been messing with Vaughn." His statement made me snap my eyes toward him. He didn't look angry or disgusted, only shocked as his round and wide eyes floated back and forth between Smoke and me.

I finally found my voice. "We didn't mean for this to…I don't want Smoke to lose everything…"

I forced my legs to move forward as Smoke looked back at me, confusion in his eyes. "I can leave or call it off," I said. "Anything to save his ass."

"Calm down," Felix said. Smoke shot me a wary glance. "No shame in being attracted to each other. I told you my brother was gay."

My shoulders relaxed as I let out a harsh breath.

"Seemed like more than that, though." Felix thumped Smoke's shoulder to force his gaze on him. "More than just screwing around. The way you were looking at him, fuck—"

Neither of us spoke as if unable to grasp at what to say, how to explain.

All of a sudden we heard the back door swing open, and we froze in place.

"You guys still here?" Jonas's voice floated over the silence, and he appeared in the doorway with some woman who was definitely not his old lady. His hair was in disarray, probably from her fingers, and a red stain of lipstick was smudged across his chin.

The very idea that Jonas could mess around on his woman, but I couldn't freely show Smoke affection in my own bar, made me want to punch the fucking wall.

"I was just driving April home and remembered that I left my key ring on the desk." When Jonas realized none of us had spoken a word, he sobered up quickly, releasing his hold on the girl. "Why so serious? Something happen?"

Whereas I felt a brief stab of relief earlier when it was Felix who'd walked in on Smoke and me, I now had the dreaded realization that he held our fate in his very hands.

The tension in the room grew thick, and I could actually hear the ticking of the clock on the back wall. And this time it was nowhere near a comfort.

Finally Felix shook his head. "Nah, man. Smoke and I were just organizing patrol tonight."

"All right, then," Jonas said, his posture sagging. "Catch you later."

None of us moved until after we heard the back door slam shut.

"Thanks, man, I—" Smoke began, but Felix cut him off.

"This thing serious between the two of you?"

Smoke stared into his eyes and finally nodded. "Yeah. Doesn't matter, though. Mal would never…"

"How do you know?" Felix asked. "Cory and Jude already softened him to the idea. Maybe it would be different for you."

"Even if it was…" Smoke said. "The other guys…"

Felix shrugged. "Who knows…they'd probably follow Mal's lead."

"Doesn't mean they'd still show Smoke the same respect when Mal wasn't around," I said, nearly desperate to fix everything, make it all right for Smoke. "Listen. *Christ*. I'm gonna leave you guys to discuss your options…"

"Don't you fucking dare," Smoke said, firmly grabbing my arm. "We're in this together, goddammit. Or at least, I thought we were."

He stared at me unflinching until my shoulders dropped and I took a step back. I was totally losing my shit. I thought I'd make it easier by leaving. But that would be walking out on Smoke, the guy I was in love with and wanted to be with. "You're right. We are."

We were two consenting adults. It shouldn't have to be this fucking hard.

"Listen, I only returned to use the restroom and tell you I was heading on patrol. Let me know when you're back home," Felix said, heading toward the door. "You guys work it out. Should be able to give whatever this is a fair shot."

"It's not as simple as that," I said, shaking my head.

"My brother was beaten up for crushing on another dude when we were kids," Felix said. "That shit is wrong. Until you make some decisions, your secret is safe with me."

After he left, we moved around the bar in dulled silence, making sure things were secure before we closed up shop. Neither one of us spoke a word, both stumbling through our own heavy thoughts.

It felt strange to alert Felix that we were safely home, because by now he'd probably put two and two together that we had been sleeping in the same bed.

Regardless, as soon as we lay down, we clung to each other like lifelines, our limbs winding and clutching, as if attempting to hang on to the last vestiges of what was once our secret refuge.

After tonight, who knew what we'd be? Except to each other.

Smoke made slow and almost melancholy love to me, the only sounds in the room our moans and breaths. His lips rarely left mine, his tongue feathering inside my mouth in an almost constant rhythm.

"I'm sorry," I whispered against his lips. "I'm all in. I'll be here for as long as you want me."

We didn't profess our feelings again, but I could see all of his emotions laid bare in his eyes. He was as worried and desperate as I was, and somehow that was a comfort. Though tonight could've been so much worse. It might've been Jonas or Mal or any of the other guys walking in on us. There had to be a ray of light in there somewhere.

CHAPTER THIRTY
SMOKE

Vaughn and I walked numbly through the next couple of days as if on eggshells because of being found out by Felix, but also with the knowledge that the Scorpions were moving in on the Asylum.

The Disciples weren't told exactly when or how the attack would go down, to keep us from being implicated. I was feeling so many warring emotions at once. Though I hoped this meant the threat to Vaughn would end, I would never want anybody to die because of it. Even my old club members, who had introduced me to drugs. I had made the decision to put the needle in my arm all by my lonesome.

But we lived by a different set of codes in the MC world. Even if Jake wasn't taken out with the rest of his club, the idea was that the Asylum's power would be weakened and they'd think twice about stealing from another organization again.

As Vaughn and I moved around each other at the bar, we barely made eye contact, both afraid of being found out. Felix acted as if everything was normal, but my stomach dropped every time Jonas or Mal looked my way.

Vaughn tried being his usual chipper and outgoing self by razzing the customers and flirting with the ladies, but it was a half-hearted attempt, and I could tell he was beginning to crack.

Once all was said and done, I was finished with hiding. This was for the birds. If my brothers wanted nothing more to do with me, I'd leave the club. I'd said as much to Vaughn this morning, while he lay on top of me in bed and pulled me into a kiss that basically curled my fucking toes. I didn't want to lose him now that I'd found him. I just didn't know exactly what that meant. Yet.

Vaughn sent Lewis and Cherry home. The back room was quiet, and still Vaughn and I didn't dare even steal a kiss on Hog's Den property. This might've been a safe haven for other people, but we were mistaken to think we were secure as well.

I was thankful nobody had walked in the night I had fucked Vaughn on the tabletop. I had been so far gone, I might not have been able to find the sense to give a shit.

"Let's go," I said, and Vaughn nodded. Neither of us spoke of him returning to his apartment in the next couple of days. We kept our bubble perfectly contained. It was sure to burst with one wrong flick of a finger.

Right as we were about to walk out, we heard a tap from the outside.

Vaughn opened the door a sliver and Sawyer from the Scorpions was standing on the other side. What in the fuck was he doing here? Jealousy and anger tightened my gut. Did he think he'd get Vaughn alone?

"Fish sent me." Sawyer looked warily over his shoulder. Maybe this was club business. "Can I come in?"

Something pricked at my brain. This didn't feel right. I swept my hand over my back pocket, feeling for my knife. I had rarely used it, though I made sure to have it with me every single day. We all did. Some of the guys still packed a gun, but most of us left them locked up in our houses now, the threats mostly gone. Or so I thought.

Vaughn looked back as I stepped up to the door, now wishing my Glock was tucked securely inside my waistband. Vaughn kept a gun in his safe here as well, but that would do us little good if this turned ugly. "What is this about?"

All of a sudden, the blur of another figure shoved past Sawyer, brandishing a nine-millimeter and aiming it at Vaughn's head.

"Stand down, Smoke," the guy growled.

I thrust my hands in the air. "What the fuck, Jake?"

Vaughn's eyes snapped to mine and then over to Jake, looking him up and down. I could see the wheels spinning in Vaughn's head. *So this is the infamous ex. The one who ruthlessly pissed in my house and poisoned my cat.*

What in the hell was Jake doing with Sawyer?

"You're brave to show your face here," I said.

"Your brothers will have other things to worry about tonight," he sneered.

Fear lanced through my heart. "What the fuck are you talking about?"

He didn't answer. Instead, he directed Sawyer to fasten Vaughn's wrists with some plastic cable ties and lead him to one of the tables. "You even move an muscle, a bullet goes through your lover's head."

"You still think he's my lover?" I bit out as Vaughn was forced into a chair in the middle of the room and Sawyer bent down to secure his ankles. I tried like hell to think of a way out of this, but Vaughn was unarmed, and it would be two against one.

And Jake was just crazy enough to pull that trigger.

As Sawyer manhandled my wrists together, I attempted to catch his eye. "You're betraying your club?"

He forced me into a chair across from Vaughn while he tied the plastic strip around my ankles. "The club that was going to kill my boyfriend?"

"Your—"

My words were halted when Jake yanked Sawyer by the front of his shirt and kissed him, his tongue practically deep-throating him.

"Mmmm...those lips," Jake murmured against his mouth. "He even gives better head than you, Smoke."

I nearly gagged on my own saliva. I stared at the back door, hoping that one of the brothers would decide to return tonight. Jonas for his keys. Felix for some water. The other night in the kitchen seemed ridiculous in comparison. I'd shout from the rooftops that I was with Vaughn if it meant keeping him alive.

Jake stood smirking in front of me, and my gaze scanned behind him to Vaughn. Our eyes met and held as I tried to convey an apology to him. He minutely shook his head as if to say it wasn't my fault. But it definitely was. I had brought Jake into his life. All because I desperately needed to be with him.

And even now, tied up across the room from him, possibly minutes before our deaths, I felt the exact same way. I loved him. Wanted to make a life with him, if only we had a decent chance. I forced my gaze away from him and back to Sawyer.

"You know that he's been stalking me?" I said, angling my head toward Jake. "The sick shit he did to Vaughn's apartment?"

"Of course Sawyer knows," Jake said, rolling his eyes. "He also knows I have unfinished business with you."

"Well, I don't have any with you," I said. "Getting clean and leaving your club was the best decision I ever made. Saved my life."

"Always so condescending," Jake hissed. "Think you got your life all figured out?"

"At least I was getting there," I said, shaking my head. "More than I can say for you. Still committing petty home invasions just for kicks? You're even high right now, aren't you?"

"Your club might not be pulling deals anymore, but you're still involved in stolen property," he said, now aiming the gun at the ground. "Still got dirty money coming in."

"You sure seem to know a lot about our business," I said, then turned my attention back to Sawyer. I needed somehow to force him off balance. "Your boyfriend tell you how he followed me out on patrol and asked me to take him back?"

Out of the corner of my eye, I noticed how Vaughn's jaw dropped, but I kept my gaze trained on Sawyer and Jake.

"He doesn't care who I fuck as long as I'm in his bed most nights," Jake said with not one ruffled feather. "We have an open relationship."

"Yeah?" I called to Sawyer, "He top you real hard when you're high, leaving his marks?"

Vaughn winced, finally understanding why I couldn't let anybody have control for the past few years. Nobody but him.

"He likes it rough, don't you, baby?" Jake asked Sawyer, who nodded slowly, his jaw ticking, either from my questions or from Jake's attention being so trained on me. "Besides, who do you think told us you were working on the inside with the Scorpions?"

I looked into Sawyer's eyes, and something unreadable shuttered in his gaze, but I couldn't quite place it. "I wouldn't want to be you when the Scorpions find out you betrayed them," I told him.

Jake reached for Sawyer's shoulder. "He won't have to worry about that anymore."

My chest felt as tight as my bound wrists. "What the hell do you mean?"

"The Scorpions and the Disciples are going down tonight."

My heart jumped to my throat as I stole a look across the room at Vaughn, who blanched. We'd been double-crossed. Fuck, I knew something was off. What the hell was Mal thinking, working with that crew?

I'd had that feeling the entire time I was helping Fish, and now it was all making sense. *Sawyer.* All because he liked being fucked by Jake.

But hadn't I been doing same thing? Practically throwing it all away because of a good lay?

Yet as I stared into Vaughn's turbulent eyes, my body flooded with different emotions. There was no shame. Only a sense of longing and protection and need.

Nah, I couldn't place myself down on their level. I wasn't betraying my club. I was only trying to chase love.

"So why are you here instead of helping your club take us out?" I choked out the words, trying to keep my brain from going numb and shutting down on me.

"I told you I had unfinished business."

CHAPTER THIRTY-ONE
SMOKE

I adjusted my wrists against the ties, hoping he'd secured them too loosely. No such luck. "What kind of unfinished business do you think we have?"

Jake's gaze swung to Sawyer, and his lips curled into a sneer. I'd seen that look directed at other people plenty of times. But now it seemed downright sinister. Like he was the devil himself.

But even the devil was vulnerable.

A familiar crinkling sound filled my eardrums, and my entire body went numb. Sawyer fished a small plastic bag from his pocket, and all of my senses went on high alert.

I didn't need to see the spoon or the cotton ball or the syringe. My trained nostrils had already picked up the faint hint of vinegar that heroin tabs produced before being dissolved into their purest form.

Saliva coated my tongue as my mouth watered. Actually fucking watered. It was like an old lover calling me to surrender. This time the lover wasn't Jake. But she was nearly as deadly as him. Fun while she lasted, leaving you as hollow as a cavern when she was through.

"Fuck, man." Vaughn's voice burst forth in a jagged pant across the room. For the first time since being tied up, Vaughn had spoken up. "Why the hell would you go messing with a man's sobriety?"

"Oh please," Jake said as he eyed the heroin crystal like it was liquid gold. And it definitely was to many of us. Until it turned your life to acid and gouged out your fucking soul. "He thinks he's better than me now that he's sober."

"No." Vaughn shook his head almost violently. "He's just trying to make a decent life for himself."

That got a good, hearty laugh out of Jake.

"Is that what this is about?" I asked, and Jake's gaze snapped to mine. "I left you because I was going to die if I didn't."

His eyes softened momentarily, and I knew I had hit on something raw. "You get that, right?" I said. "It wasn't you. It was the drugs."

"If it was the drugs, then why not come back to me after you got sober?"

My gaze swung briefly to Sawyer, who stood staring with his mouth hanging open. I couldn't allow my eyes to search for Vaughn's. I hoped he understood that I was trying anything I could to save our lives. I would never in a million years feel for Jake how I felt for him. Vaughn was everything and Jake was nothing.

"I had to go through the program twice, Jake," I said. "And even now, it's hard to be near…near…"

I couldn't even say the name of the drug that had wrecked my life. I was weakened by her very presence in the room.

A smile tugged at his mouth. "You still crave it, don't you?"

He watched me closely until I nodded. "In the program, they teach you not to be around it anymore. Or anybody who uses it."

"Me," he said, as if finally understanding.

"You."

We stared each other down, and I thought maybe I had gotten through to him, until there was movement beside us. Sawyer had produced a lighter from his pocket, and Jake's gaze darkened against the flicker of flame.

I watched as his eyes turned nearly black. He stepped toward Sawyer, kissed him, and motioned to the lighter. When he looked back at me one final time, I knew I had lost him again. Probably for good.

Sawyer's gaze shifted wildly to the door as if somebody would come busting through to find them at any minute. Fuck, I hoped against hope that his fears turned to reality.

As Sawyer positioned the flame beneath the rounded plastic, nothing could force my gaze away from that white goddess, now lying in wait on a spoon.

My entire body shuddered from the vivid memory of how she inhabited my brain, ravaged my veins. I looked down at my elbow, attempting to find the best entryway in the crook of my arm, nearly ravenous for her.

I could envision the track marks on my skin, the purple and yellow bruising, now faded with time. If I ran my finger over the sensitive area, I'd still feel the knobs of scar tissue, some of which were visible to the naked eye. My forehead became slick with sweat, and a couple of drops trickled onto my lap.

"You remember this beauty," Jake said, gaping at me. "How she makes you feel?"

"No," I said, nearly strangling on the syllable, but still keeping my gaze trained on her.

"Oh yeah, baby," he said, pushing my hair away from my eyes, like he used to do. "You're going to beg me for her."

"Never," I rasped, but I knew I was already fighting a losing battle.

"You will. You're going to skyrocket to the moon, and then I'm going to fuck you while you fuck Sawyer." I yanked my head away from Jake and his fingers moved to Sawyer's hair instead, playing him like a finely tuned violin. "Isn't that right, baby?"

Sawyer looked between the two of us and nodded. In my peripheral vision I could see the chair tilting across the room as Vaughn struggled to get loose.

"Shoot me up instead." Vaughn's tortured voice struck a chord deep in my soul. "You fucking animal. If you ever felt anything for Smoke, you'd cut him this break."

Jake threw his head back and laughed. "Why, so you can get fucked by me instead?"

"Do whatever the hell you want to me," he said. "Just make sure that heroin goes in my bloodstream instead."

"Vaughn—" I cried out.

"Shut the fuck up, Smoke," he growled, and I when searched his face, I saw a conviction there I'd never seen in another lover's eyes before. Or probably would ever again. "Not another word."

"Maybe it would be fun to see why Smoke likes fucking you so much," Jake said, watching our exchange. "Or do you fuck him…hmmm?"

"Shoot me up instead of him and find out how good I can be," Vaughn said, and I squeezed my eyes shut so tight I was seeing stars. Vaughn was taking up for me, being so fucking brave. I was determined not to look in the direction of that spoon again.

"Might have a good time with that one," Sawyer drawled, and I wanted to punch the motherfucker in the face. What had Fish ever done to make him want to betray him like this? To me, his offense was way worse than Jake's. At least Jake had been an asshole from the onset.

"You're both going to die tonight," Jake said. "So what does it matter whether your brain is addled or not?"

"Smoke has a lot to be proud of," Vaughn said, slouching in his seat. "At least let him keep his dignity. He worked so fucking hard to achieve his sobriety."

I had a gigantic lump in my throat, because we were more than likely not getting out of this alive. It sounded like none of the Disciples were, either. At least if I was going to die, I was doing it knowing somebody cared for me that fucking much. I hoped he knew it, too.

"Vaughn," I said, my eyes frantically searching his, wanting to convey everything I was thinking. Feeling. For him. Only him. No way I wanted these motherfuckers to be our audience, but this moment was all that we had.

Vaughn's raw emotions were written all over his face—he was flayed open, laid bare to me. All of our hopes and dreams down the drain, only anger and fear and love—deep and desperate and tragic love—remained between us. So visceral I could practically taste it in my mouth.

"Will you look at this, Sawyer?" Jake said, nudging him. "A pair of bartenders who like fucking each other. Right beneath Mal's nose."

"You've been screwing behind the scenes this entire time," I spit out. "Terrence isn't wondering why you've taken such an interest in me tonight?"

His jaw ticked. "I told him I wanted to kill you myself. That you burned me good after I took you in, helped you out."

"You call that helping me out?"

He looked around the space as if for the first time, taking in the fixtures on the wall, and zeroing in on one of my welded pieces. "You miss having a bar to call your own, Smoke?"

"You know I do." There was a spark in my peripheral vision as Sawyer flicked the lighter one final time. A cotton ball would soak the liquid up like a sponge and filter out any particles so that the syringe could work its magic. Though I kept my eyes trained on my feet, I was practically tilting my chair toward the flame now.

"Too bad your uncle took that from you."

"My uncle?" My eyes darted toward Jake. "Because he got the insurance money?"

"How do you think he arranged that?"

"What the fuck are you talking about?"

"He wanted the money," Jake jerked his shoulder. "And I wanted you."

I thought about how Jake would come up to the bar when I worked with my father. How he'd make small talk with me. And then when he approached me after the fire. How I was so distressed and alone. How my uncle skirted town directly after the funeral.

"You saying my uncle committed arson?"

"I'm not saying anything," Jake told me on a yawn. As if he hadn't just tilted my entire world on its fucking axis.

"The way I heard it," Sawyer said, watching the cotton ball soak up the heroin, "you were too wasted to follow up on any police leads, anyway."

I lifted my bound feet and kicked at his shin, hard enough that he nearly dropped the spoon.

"Gotten feisty, haven't you?" Jake spun on me and grabbed me by the collar, so we were nose to nose. "There's the spark I saw when I first met you."

"Hard to keep the spark going when you're always high," I said, practically spitting in his face. "Maybe that's what Jake's doing to you right now, Sawyer. Ever think of that? If I were you, I'd watch my back."

"Enough of this bullshit," Sawyer growled. "Let's shoot him up already, fuck him raw, and then torch this place down."

I held in my gasp, but Vaughn said the words for me. "Why does this place need to be torched?"

"Got a tie to the joint, huh?" Jake barked out a laugh, his saliva flying in my face. "How else we gonna destroy the evidence?"

"C'mon, we've got enough to shoot both of them up," Sawyer said, shoving the lighter back in his pocket.

I grimaced, barely keeping it together. "You guys won't be joining us?"

"Aw, how sweet, worrying about us," Jake said. "You liked it when I fucked you high, didn't you?"

I shuddered, and Jake's grin was so devious he could've grown horns right then.

Jake approached Vaughn, and I bit so hard into my lip that I tasted blood.

"How about only you and me take the two hits?" Vaughn said, and I could see his fingers trembling as he tried one last time to reason with Jake. "You show me what you got."

"I'm going to enjoy shooting up your boyfriend, Smoke," Jake said, petting Vaughn's hair. "Especially since he asked for it."

"No!" I watched as Vaughn squirmed and resisted the needle. As Jake squeezed the plunger, sending the heroin into his bloodstream, his eyes rolled in the back in his head. Saliva gushed to my mouth as I remembered the sensation of that first high. I wanted to feel it, too, so fucking much, my teeth were chattering.

I loathed myself for needing it so desperately.

Jake whistled as he stared at Vaughn, whose mouth had gone slack. "That good, baby?"

My eyes filled with tears as I looked at my lover's face, his eyes glassy and dilated. "You fucking bastard."

"Let's get this show on the road," Sawyer said, and he stepped toward me with the second syringe.

Sawyer angled the needle at my skin as panic and eagerness warred heavily in my chest. He laid the syringe against my vein and then looked me dead in the eye.

It was as if the sound had been blotted out of the room. I could hear my heartbeat thundering in my ears. One, two, three seconds ticked by.

"Fall," he whispered in my ear a moment before my chair was toppled over and I smacked the floor hard.

Then all hell broke loose as shouts arose from the back of the room. A shot whizzed past my ear as I crawled sloppily toward Vaughn with bound limbs. My eyesight fuzzed and my breathing was labored as I zeroed in on saving the man I loved. I threw my body on top of him to protect him from any stray bullets.

When I next looked up at the bar, Mal was standing over Jake, pummeling his face into a bloody pulp. A line of blood dribbled from his nose onto the front of his shirt.

"You just had to go and mess with one of our own. You stupid motherfucker," he said. "You and your club are finished."

He gave a brusque nod to Sawyer, who angled the Glock straight at Jake's heart, the silencer screwed expertly in place, and delivered the fatal blow.

CHAPTER THIRTY-TWO
VAUGHN

I felt warm, fleshy lips breathing against my mouth, and I groaned into the feathery kiss. Smoke's tongue traced my lips, just a swipe, but oh, so incredible to feel him, all of him, since only a few days ago, we were both as good as dead.

Smoke had stood vigilant over me since that night, wondering if my side effects might send me into the deep end, whether I'd want to seek out another hit. Sure, that dose of heroin had knocked me on my ass like a runaway train. It was like thirty minutes of pure unadulterated nirvana, but coming down scared the living shit out of me.

But now I got it. How it was so addicting and appealing. How Smoke seemed to beg Sawyer not only with his eyes but his entire body when it was directly in front of him. It was the type of high I had never encountered before. I would certainly never forget it. I also never wanted to experience it again for as long as I lived.

Smoke had asked me to describe it. My mood, sensations, perceptions, as he helplessly sat watching me across the room.

Then he promptly went out and found himself an NA meeting. After he got home, he never asked me about it again.

His hands smoothed over my chest, heading down to my stomach. My fingers reached to feel for him. He was rock hard and still completely naked, even though the scent of our morning coffee drifted toward my nose.

"When are we leaving?"

Mal had asked us out to the compound today. It would be the first time I'd seen him since the other night. He'd called to check on us several times, and he got regular reports from Felix.

The Disciples had an emergency meeting the day after Jake was killed to talk about what went down that night. The entire Asylum club had been decimated by the Scorpions and Russians. Sawyer obviously had been ordered to work both sides and played his part expertly.

But we still didn't know what that meant for Smoke and me. And at this point, it didn't even matter.

"Not for another hour," Smoke said as his fingers slid around my erection. "We've still got time."

"Come here," I mumbled, wanting to feel his smooth body over mine, the weight of his chest. His heartbeat as he lay on top of me. Pulse to pulse, skin to skin, cock to cock. This was the only drug I needed.

"No matter what happens today," he said roughly against my ear, "it'll always be you, Vaughn. For me."

"Mmmm…" I hummed as my hand sealed around his nape and I pulled his lips to mine, showing him exactly how much he meant to me.

"We'll make it work," I said, tilting his chin. "Whatever that means."

"What you did for me the other night…" he said, his voice watery as emotions crept across his face in waves. "That was…"

"Shhhh…I love you," I whispered against his mouth. "And I'd do it again every single time. You protected me, too. The way you covered me when the bullets started flying?"

His kiss was rough, passionate. "I need to be inside you."

Our cocks rubbed and slicked together, and my eyes flickered shut as a shiver worked through me. "I want to feel you raw. Nothing between us."

At the insistence of Mal, Smoke and I had been thoroughly examined after that night. It was by a doctor who was on their payroll and off the record. While we were at it, we asked for additional testing and had both received a clean bill of health.

Smoke watched me intently for a long moment before he nodded and groaned, lining up his cock. "I won't last the first time."

As I raised my knees and he nudged inside me, everything gleamed like the sharp edge on the blade of a knife. In that moment, it was only Reed and me. And everything was right, amazing, unblemished in our own little sanctuary.

How this perfection could ever be questioned in the world outside of us, I didn't know.

"Oh goddamn—" he moaned. "I can't even…uuuuuhhhhh."

He changed position, hitting that one spot inside me, and my nerve endings caught on fire. "Oh fuck, I can feel you, really feel you. Incredible."

I clutched my own cock and pumped myself into oblivion, my seed spurting in ribbons all over my chest and neck.

"Don't close your eyes," he said as my legs shook and my head lolled side to side. "I want to watch you."

My eyes flashed open and our gazes collided. He bent his head to lick come off my neck before he kissed my lips. His tongue slid against mine and I tasted myself. "Gorgeous."

His thrusts became more ragged as his mouth fell open in a silent groan. As he came, I looked into his vividly green eyes and saw him in his purest state, laid bare to me. His truest, rawest form. Perfection.

"Oh fuck, can you feel that?" he said, quivering. "It's like we're mixed together inside you now."

Words had escaped me. So I reached up and touched his flawless lips, his flushed and trembling chest, and I knew that I would never feel this way for anybody else again. This resounding toll in the deepest recesses of my soul was reserved only for him.

CHAPTER THIRTY-THREE
VAUGHN

We rode out to the compound together, both wondering if this was where the big boom would come down. Though I no longer felt like I needed to look over my shoulder, there were so many unanswered questions, and none of the guys were talking.

Not even Felix, who told us to speak to the prez first, though he seemed more than relieved that we'd made it out alive.

The compound was quiet when we arrived. Nobody was around except for Jonas.

Smoke and I had decided that no matter what, we were done hiding, and we'd do what it took to be together. I'd break the news to my father, hoping in time he'd come to accept it. I'd dealt with my sexuality my whole life. Even I didn't understand it. I just knew it was who I was. I should've told him sooner.

Mal was sitting at his desk, scrolling through his laptop, while Jonas finished up a phone call. Smoke and I sat down a bit awkwardly, neither seeming to know what to do or say.

Jonas ended his phone call and after a long, drawn-out silence, Mal finally cleared his throat. "You think I didn't suspect anything?"

My stomach dropped out. I parted my lips, attempting to suck air through my lungs.

"I waited for you, Smoke," he said. "To tell me you and Vaughn were together, or were trying to work through some things, or what the fuck *ever,* but you never came clean."

Mal didn't seem furious, more like annoyed and even somewhat amused. Like we had tried to pull the wool over his eyes and didn't succeed. But it hadn't been like that at all.

"I never set out to disappoint you. Not after everything you've done for me." Smoke grabbed hold of his cut as if ready to slide it over his shoulders. "If you want to send me packing, I can—"

"The fuck?" Mal's voice boomed through the space, and I flinched. "Do you really have such a low opinion of me?"

I didn't dare open my mouth. This was really between Smoke and Mal. Almost like brother to brother, even father to son.

"Fuck, no. I didn't know how to have him in my life and be faithful to you, too," Smoke said, straightening in the chair, his hands falling to his sides. "It's not like I set out to feel this way for Vaughn. In fact, I tried to fight it. For a long time."

"We both did," I murmured, looking at my boots. "But I can't be sorry for my feelings for him. Only that we didn't tell you sooner."

I could hear Jonas breathing heavily next to me. I couldn't even deal with how he was feeling right then, so I averted my gaze.

One fire at a time.

"The reason I had Vaughn stay with you these past few weeks?" Mal said, up and pacing now. "That was because I knew *you* would protect him best. Understand?"

I gaped. He'd had his suspicions even then on how we felt about each other. Smoke looked over at me, his eyes wide, his fingers making the motion to reach for my hand, but keeping himself in check at the last minute.

"Now," Mal continued, rushing his fingers through his hair. "You kept some things from me and I did the same, for a larger reason."

Both of our heads sprang up to meet his eyes. Mal threw a look at Jonas that was a cross between bummed and disappointed.

"I'm talking about Fish and me plotting with Sawyer to get closer to Jake," he said. "I figured you guys knowing would make our plan less authentic. I'm sorry about that, but I stand by that decision."

Smoke swallowed thickly. He threw me a glance, and I rolled my shoulder. After all was said and done, the way things went down was cool by me. We were all safe and alive. I wouldn't pretend to know all of Mal's reasons for not keeping Smoke in the loop, but I didn't want to analyze it now.

"From now on, I need us all to be on the up and up," he said. "You feel me?"

Smoke bit his lip and nodded. "You have my word."

Mal held out his hand for Smoke to shake on it.

When he grasped for my hand, he patted me on the back. "There will most likely be some growing pains with the other guys. But I'm confident it'll all work out. We didn't come this far to get derailed by a brother falling in love."

Smoke kept his head down, his knee bouncing a mile a minute, his jaw working his gum.

I could feel my neck heat up as Jonas added his two cents. "Hear hear."

Mal sat down on the edge of his desk and reached for a large manila envelope that he handed to Smoke.

"What's this?" Smoke said, turning it over in his hand.

"Open it," Mal said, waiting for Smoke to unclasp the envelope. "The Hog's Den will be closed for another week while we make some changes."

My eyebrows drew together. "Changes?"

He shrugged. "New paint on the walls, maybe some new chairs. Whatever you decide."

Smoke stared at the documents on his lap. "I don't understand."

"I'm giving you the option to buy me out," he said. "I'll still maintain a small share. But the Hog's Den is yours if you want it."

What the hell was happening here?

Using his finger as a placeholder, Smoke looked up from the line he was attempting to focus on. "Buy you out? I can't afford…what the fuck…why?"

"You tell me if I'm wrong. But deep down I figure it's what you really want," he said. "Your family's business was taken away from you at an early age."

Smoke shook his head as if to clear the cobwebs. "My uncle?"

"We finally found the bastard," he said and stole a quick look at me. "And let's just say…he did the right thing."

"Took some persuasion," Jonas added and I cringed, not really wanting to know what that meant.

"He fucked up and he knows it," Mal said. "Gave you enough money to cover my portion of the bar."

Closing his eyes on an inhalation, Smoke sank lower in his seat. "So it's true? He was after the insurance money?"

Mal patted Smoke's shoulder. "We've all got people in our lives who don't deserve to be called family. You've had a shit hand dealt, for sure. Now it's time to have something of your own."

Smoke's eyes clouded with turmoil. "What about the club?"

"If you still choose to be part of our brotherhood, that's cool by me and Jonas, and all of the brothers," he said. "By a unanimous vote."

He gasped and sat up ramrod straight in the chair.

"Or you can choose to run the bar with Vaughn as is, and we'd still see you every day."

Smoke sat silent for a long while, as if weeding through everything that had been said.

"I could never repay you for—" Smoke choked out the words.

"You repay me by being happy."

* * *

It'd been a couple of weeks since the shootout. I was sweeping the floor at the Hog's Den, prepping for our grand reopening. We ignored the grumble of the regulars who complained that they liked the space just fine as is. Little did they know that their favorite barstools had been close to becoming a pile of ash that one night.

Lewis and Cherry had accepted our news without even flinching. Cherry had said she'd already suspected something was up between me and Smoke. Lewis was simply Lewis. Nothing really fazed him.

Smoke and I didn't have it all figured out yet. Outside of new paint, we chose not to do anything drastically different with the bar. There'd been enough change in our lives for the moment and besides, why mess with a good thing?

I had briefly returned to my apartment and let my landlord know that I wouldn't be re-signing the lease. Smoke was still feeling his way around after taking a walk from the club. Most of the brothers had given us their blessing.

Smoke drove over to my pop's house with me the other night with a peace offering of sorts. He had crafted an unusual-looking clock from some vintage auto parts, and I loved watching my dad's eyes light up when he saw that thing.

After he left, I stayed and broke the news to my pop, who took the idea of Smoke and me building a life together better that I expected. Mary was present, which I'd admit helped lessen the blow. They had begun seeing each other on a regular basis, and she was good for him.

Smoke appeared from the back room wearing his Hog's Den T-shirt. The material clung to his chest in all the right places, and I wanted to push him down on the bar top and have my way with him. But we had set some ground rules. No more fooling around at our place of business. Still, I couldn't help stealing a kiss or two every hour, at least.

"You ready?" Smoke asked, interlacing our fingers.

"As I'll ever be," I said, raising his hand to kiss his palm.

Smoke reached up to clang the new bell above the bar, similar to one his dad had used at Mitsy's place, he'd said. He even had the brass engraved with his mother's name.

"What do you think?" I asked, enjoying the sound as much as the gleam in his eye.

"I think I'm happy," he said, his rough hands clutching my jaw. "I think I finally found what I've been searching for."

Thump. Thump. Thump.

Our lips met, and my tongue dipped inside his mouth. We kissed long and slow and deep, my fingers digging into his waist, with the promise of so much more.

But it would have to wait. We had a bar to run tonight.

Smoke's lips skimmed across my ear. "I think I definitely found home."

THANK YOU for reading THE DARKEST FLAME!

I hope you enjoyed it!

Reviews help other readers find books. So if you feel compelled one way or another to leave a review, I appreciate it!

Read on to view a short excerpt from **THERE YOU STAND**, Cory and Jude's book.

ACKNOWLEDGEMENTS

To my agent, Sara Megibow—for always supporting me and believing in my books, especially when I can't see the forest through the trees. It means more than you can imagine.

To the team who helped make this book shine: Bev Katz Rosenbaum, for the developmental edits, and the Formatting Fairies for the copyedits and proofing. You rock. Kanaxa, for my amazing cover, and Nina Bocci, for not only being an amazing publicist but a kick-ass friend.

To Stina, Kate, and Deb: Thank you for dropping everything to read for me and then giving me crucial feedback.

To my family and friends for your constant, unwavering support. I love you.

To Greg and Evan, for not complaining when I have to disappear to work at odd hours of any random day. I don't want to be in any other place in the world except right next to you, every single night.

To the amazing book bloggers and reviewers out there—there are too many of you to list here. Please just know I appreciate all the work you do—all on your own dime—for the simple love of books. Because when it comes down to it, all of us are readers first and foremost.

Last, to the readers: THANK YOU for taking a chance on my books and reaching out to talk to me about them. For an author, there may be no better feeling.

ABOUT THE AUTHOR

Once upon a time, I lived in New York City and was a wardrobe stylist. I spent my days getting in cabs, shopping for photo shoots, eating amazing food, and drinking coffee at my favorite hangouts.

Now I live in the Midwest with my husband and son—my two favorite guys. I've been a clinical social worker and a special education teacher. But it wasn't until I wrote a weekly column for the local newspaper that I realized I could turn the fairytales inside my head into the reality of writing fiction.

I'm addicted to lip gloss and salted caramel everything. I believe in true love and kissing, so writing romance novels has become a dream job.

I write Adult, New Adult, and M/M Contemporary Romance. I also own a hand-stamped jewelry business, which requires me to stamp letters and/or words onto pieces of silver. They go hand-in-hand perfectly.

Excerpt from
There You Stand

I swallowed past the lump in my throat and leaned over to pat Chopper, the dog I'd inherited a couple of months ago from Joe, my latest asshole boyfriend. The dude skipped town without him and I didn't have it in me to drive him to the pound.

What a damn sucker I was, because the mutt had a mind of his own, didn't obey commands for shit, and was demanding as hell. He got along well with my older dog, Ace, when he wasn't jockeying for position and trying to hog all the attention. Damn needy pain in the ass.

He was getting restless while I was stopped to take another swig from my water bottle. This had become my morning routine. I'd walk Chopper and Ace a couple of miles around town and always end up at Washington Park. My eyes couldn't help but wander to the bowl, where the skaters from the hood hung out. And without fail my gaze was immediately drawn to him.

Like a damn weed to the sun. Because I'd give my left nut that Jude York was as straight as they come.

I whistled through my teeth as his lean and hard body sailed high, his knees bent in flawless formation. He landed smoothly on the far wall of the ramp, his skateboard gliding effortlessly along the curved cement.

My back was on fire again, so I readjusted myself on the uncomfortable wooden bench. Staying past last call at the bar would do that to you. At least that's what I told myself. But deep down I knew it was due to my injury, which would always be a bleak reminder of that one tragic night.

Ignoring the discomfort, my gaze again slid beyond the statuesque trees. Jude was beautiful when he rode. Graceful and strong, the muscles in his legs taut as he climbed those hills. I never noticed him talking to the other skaters, other than with a nod, as if it was an unspoken agreement that he was simply there to do his thing.

I had no clue whether or not he knew that I watched. Might kick my ass if he found out. I always had my dogs with me, so it was a decent excuse. I'd sit on this bench, hide behind my dark shades and trusty knit cap, and refill my water bottle at the fountain behind me.

Rumor had it that Jude moved here to make a fresh start. Others said he was hiding from his past. I'd seen him around for months now, either skating in the bowl or working in the back of the shop at the Board Room. Most recently he had walked into Raw Ink, and scrolled through the portfolios in our waiting room, considering a new addition to his ink.

I'd walked a customer up front that afternoon, my gaze immediately drawn to his long fingers, rough calluses, as they flipped through the pages. Jessie gave me a look from behind the front counter. A look that told me she was just as intrigued.

Dex, another tattoo artist who spent one too many nights at the local bars, said he heard Jude was a transplant from out west. Said there was talk of a secret past, maybe some jail time, though he was hard- pressed to find anybody who had actually spoken to the guy.

Could be because Jude was quiet, kept to himself, and rarely made eye contact. But the combo of his dreads and sleeves of ink made him look threatening—hard around the edges—and that made some folks around here anxious. Add the fact that there was a darkness in his eyes, and that he seemed almost hyperaware of his surroundings. People figured he had a lot to hide.

But I didn't see it that way. Maybe he didn't want anyone to get close, so he performed the part. I played a role, too. After David left me three years ago, I applied for the job at Raw Ink. So little did Jude know, his darkness—which I assumed must be rooted in a pain similar to mine—only drew me nearer.

Besides, I could only imagine what had been said around town about me. I was openly gay, but understood all too well about keeping secrets. I figured Jude was a decent but silent guy, and had good reason for it.

At least that was the fantasy I kept about him in my head. Fuck, I was pathetic. But plenty of straight boys had filled my deluded brain over the years, none nearly as mysterious as him.

Hadn't I learned early on that it was impossible to bend a straight arrow? Especially if you didn't want that arrow to pierce your heart?

I bolted up on that thought, not wanting to feel as needy as this damn dog. Or hard up for that matter. There was plenty of fresh meat around this town anyway. Just not the kind I wanted or needed. Not anymore.

Chopper was thrilled that we were on the move again and he tugged hard on the lead. "Easy, boy. Let me get my these leashes untangled."

But as he lunged away from me, the leash cut across my shin and I tripped over the taut line, releasing my grip. Suddenly Chopper broke from my grasp and began running free. Fucker was going to get himself run over by a damn car someday. "Chopper, get your ass back here!"

At the sound of my voice, he looked behind him, his tongue wagging in an almost taunting smile. Then he kept on sailing free. Ace was barking and going ballistic beside me, so I tightened my hold on his line. As I began gaining on Chopper, my only hope was that he'd stop of his own volition.

Halfway across the grassy field, he spotted a squirrel in one of the trees and went wild, climbing halfway up the trunk, jumping and barking.

While he was distracted, I silently moved toward him, hoping to grab hold of that leash. But just as I approached, he took off again, following that same squirrel who'd taken a leap to the next large maple.

I was out of breath and now beyond frustrated. Remembering the treats in my pocket, I figured I could lure him as my final option—and it was now fast approaching. I shoved my hand in my hoodie, my fingers closing on a sturdy dog cookie.

When I looked up again, Chopper was headed straight for the skate park.

"Chopper, goddamn it," I called in some last-ditch effort. "You don't listen for shit." Unexpectedly, Jude neared the cement barrier at the entrance to the bowl. His board clutched in his fist, he seemed to be assessing the situation as the large dog charged nearer.

He left his board on the concrete walkway and stepped into the lawn. He squatted down in the grass, made eye contact with Chopper, and the dog changed course to sail directly toward him. What the hell was that about?

Some type of deep whistle emitted from Jude's lips and instead of slamming into his chest, Chopper came to a sudden halt beside him. Like Jude was a damn dog whisperer or something. His strong fingers grabbed hold of his collar and he reached down to mutter something in the dog's ear. Chopper sat down in the grass. Actually fucking sat down—I had never been able to get him to do that.

I became motionless as I watched them, even though Ace was eager to inch closer. At least one animal heeded my command. I wondered what it was about Jude that compelled Chopper to run toward him. I mean, I got the appeal, so maybe it was just pure animal instinct.

Except only a minute ago, Chopper was attempting to roam free, not be detained. The muscles in Jude's forearm flexed as he stroked Chopper's head and the dog's tongue hung out in a happy pant. The little fucker.

I forced my legs forward because I needed to bring Chopper back home. I had a shift at Raw Ink in an hour. And besides, Jude had done enough. I couldn't help wonder what made him come to my aid. Was he an animal lover? Did he have pets of his own?

As I walked closer to Chopper, Jude's eyes lifted to mine. And for the first time I saw an array of other emotions alight in them. The most blatant being amusement, as if his irises contained a flicker of light. His lips tilted at the corners in an almost imperceptible smile and he looked so dazzling right then. As he held my gaze for the first time ever, something tightened like a fist inside my chest.

Shit, he was stunning. In that exotic kind of way. His hair was a mass of short blond dreadlocks, his skin inked mainly in black, and his eyes were the most gorgeous light green I'd ever seen—almost like cellophane. And now those same eyes locked on mine and held steady.

"What the hell are you doing, crazy dog?" I asked Chopper, reluctantly forcing my gaze away from Jude. "I'm sorry, man."

Jude shook his head as if to say *no problem*. Even now, in this casual, inane situation, he was unwilling to speak. Had I not heard all the rumors, I might've thought that he was a mute. But Jessie assured me that he in fact had a voice. Used it to ask about a tattoo. But she'd said he was a man of few words.

I sprang into action because he was still holding on to my dog. What the hell was wrong with me?

"Chopper," I reprimanded, kneeling down at his level. "Do that again and I'll ship your ass back to your original owner."

When Jude arched his eyebrow, I couldn't help the junk that spewed from my mouth. The mouth he was now staring intently at. "My ex's dog. Left town for a new job and didn't take Chopper with him. What kind of guy does that? Anyway, wouldn't return my calls. I didn't have the balls to place him up for adoption."

Jude's eyebrows slammed together at my revelation. He was either perplexed that I'd had a boyfriend or that the guy had abandoned his dog.

When Ace cautiously stepped forward to sniff at Jude, he reached out with ease to scratch behind my other dog's ears. I continued blathering because I couldn't help myself. "This is Ace. Had him since he's been a pup."

He nodded and then opened his hand to allow Ace to lick his palm.

"You look like you're pretty used to dogs," I said. "What was that thing you did—that noise you made?—calmed Chopper right down."

He shrugged, not meeting my gaze. A line of red crawled across his neck, as if embarrassed that I'd pointed it out.

"What I mean is, you seem like a natural," I said. "Must have a dog of your own."

His eyes snapped to mine and I saw a flicker of pain there, so brief, I might've even imagined it.

"None of my business," I stammered, standing to my full height. "Thanks for helping out."

He stood up, tipped his chin, and took a step back.

"I'd still be chasing him if it wasn't for you," I said, begging my brain to get my mouth to shut the fuck up. But silence had always been hard for me. I've always felt the need to fill up any quiet lags. That way my mind wouldn't have the opportunity to go there, to that dark place. "He could've been clipped by a board or a car."

Something changed in his eyes at that comment. Something that looked like sadness and regret. Like he could identify with that scenario in some way. His mouth opened as if to say something, but then he held himself back.

My heart was thrashing in my chest. Did he have a story of his own to share?

But then the moment passed and I realized I had kept him long enough. But damn if I didn't want to linger longer. I had never been this close to him and I wanted to know more. To know everything. A ridiculous wish for sure.

He bent across the dog to hand me Chopper's leash. As I took it, our fingers brushed, and I felt a jolt of electricity. I inhaled sharply and stared at him. His expression hadn't changed but I noticed how his chest moved up and down at a quicker pace.

Could he have felt that, too? Now I was just dreaming.

I tugged at Chopper's leash and reluctantly turned to walk the dogs out of the park. "Thanks again," I threw over my shoulder.

"You're quite welcome." The shock of hearing his voice made me stop in my tracks. Not only because it was deep and rumbly, but also because it was distinctly British, and I was so not expecting that. "Aren't you an artist at Raw Ink?"

I turned to face him again, trying like hell not to stare at his full lips. "Yeah. The name's Cory. Saw you in the waiting room the other day."

He gave a curt nod, like he was unwilling to say anything more. And instead of creating another situation where I'd need to put my foot in my mouth, I turned and kept walking. My mind flashed to the day he'd been in the shop. I had never introduced myself to him. In fact, he never even looked up from the portfolios. But somehow he'd been paying attention.

"Cory," I heard him mutter.

I sucked in a breath and twisted to look back once more. I wanted to see those eyes. But he was already walking away. I watched as he picked up his board, jumped astride, and rolled across the pavement away from me.

CPSIA information can be obtained at www.ICGtesting.com
Printed in the USA
LVOW10s2218220915

455345LV00015B/193/P

9 781516 839957